I0760742

The Storyteller in the Park

JESSICA LYN ELKINS

Everfield Press
Everfieldpress.com
19005 SW 13th Avenue
Newberry Florida

ISBN:978-1-946785-05-3
ISBN-13: 978-1-946785-05-3

DEDICATION

For my grandchildren

CONTENTS

THE BEGINNING:

Once upon a time, no, it will be thrice upon a time because this story is about three people hearing stories from three storytellers. As in classic fanciful tales, the truth is never known or explained until the reader comes to a conclusion about what has really happened, what is real, or what is magical. We all want magic in our lives, but we also want truth. Truth is, a storyteller is the best way to learn—no deep thinking, no pondering, only listening to the story.

1

DAY ONE – MONDAY

ALICE

Each morning Alice left her apartment and ran across the street into the large city park. It was early fall and her class at City College did not begin until ten o'clock. She planned her schedule so that she would always have time for a long morning run.

Since coming to the city to pursue studies in urban planning, she found the routine not only necessary, but the only way she would stay sane in her new environment. Before she left her apartment, she looked in the bathroom mirror and was shocked at the face staring back at her. With dark circles under her hazel eyes, her brunette hair messily tied in a loose ponytail and the mismatched clothes she wore, the whole effect gave her the look of a stressed-out grad student which she was. She'd lost weight in the last few weeks and the loss made her look even taller than the 5'9" that she measured at her most recent physical.

Alice imagined that her continued education toward a career would be enhanced if she actually lived in an urban area. She was accepted to the Graduate Institute for Urban Planning and awarded a small research stipend due to her summa cum laude graduation from a small but nationally respected college.

The reality of living in a metropolis had not been what she expected. She'd hoped it would be exciting to interact and observe people on a daily basis while living in a walk-up apartment building that rented almost exclusively to grad students. After two months in classes, no one seemed to want to meet her and she wondered what it would take to make new friends. Her efforts to smile and greet fellow students in the lobby as they rushed off presumably to classes and part-time jobs left her depressed about the whole scene. Reserved and quiet, she always waited for others to reach out to her. She did not know how to initiate a friendship or start a conversation.

Alice's world seemed to be closing in on her.

Claustrophobia and agoraphobia were irrational fears and she suffered from both. She felt overwhelmed by the tall buildings. The crowded streets and markets made her nervous. An escape from her fears became the early morning run. She knew it was beneficial for her nature loving soul to run though the winding paths past open meadow areas and stands of large gnarled trees. The park followed the East River for several miles and made the time outdoors pleasant for her. Growing up in the Midwest far from any major waterways she had never seen the many different types of boats, tugs, and shipping vessels gliding along at steady speeds on a wide river. She loved breathing the smell of the water, even though she thought it probably too polluted for swimming or fishing. Occasionally, she saw families of ducks or other water fowl bobbing behind the wakes of small boats. Alice's morning run seemed to be the only routine that kept her from slipping into a deeper depression about two bad choices; the first was her graduate major, and the second was her decision to move to the big city.

Alice started her jog slowly, beginning on the sidewalk in front of the red brick eight- story apartments that had been built in the last century. For her, the whole block of apartments was an example of urban planning gone bad around the 1960s. Yet in her studies so far at the graduate level, she saw plans that seemed to stifle people even more: vast spaces with no real landscaping or natural features, highways intersecting neighborhoods and cutting off traditional patterns of travel. Present day planners seemed intent on the creation of clusters of buildings that belonged in a futuristic landscape made for either robots or people who stayed indoors most of their lives.

Alice set off this Monday morning in a particularly bad mood discouraged because of an experience at her part-time job the day before. She believed that applying for the job at the mall had been a good idea. She wanted to work with thriving green plants. A large nearby mall complex included extravagant plant areas close to several large fountains and benches. She saw a small advertisement for the job in the window of the management office of the mall when she dropped in to shop for a warmer jogging hat. The manager hired her on the spot. At first, she loved the experience of watering, trimming and fertilizing the many exotic plants; however, lately some of the more established plants showed signs of stress. After several days of adjusted water amounts and fertilizers, she contacted the supervisor in the management office. To her dismay, the instructions were to toss the plants in large dumpsters at the back of the mall. The plants would be replaced at the end of the month. It depressed her even more to admit there was no solution but to trash the formerly lush plants. The image had bothered her all night. When she awoke early, the idea stuck in her head that the plants were like her dreams of a career, fading and struggling because of a hostile environment and lack of proper nutrients. Maybe the only solution was to completely throw away her plans of graduate studies in urban planning, but then what?

Alice planned a different route this particular morning, hoping it would give her a better perspective of the layout of the park. She previously studied the most recent official park map and located major paths and landmarks such as a newly constructed basketball court and a wading pond for children. She found all parts of the park she explored so far to be well-used by other runners and early morning walkers. She longed for more undisturbed nature and fewer people jostling along the paths. Most of them were never smiling, super intent on their own private thoughts or hooked up to ear buds that blocked out all other sounds except their personal playlists. Did that seriously muscled younger man who looked so grim listen to a voice telling him to be confident and reach for his dreams? Or, did he listen to Beethoven's Fifth Symphony thundering into his brain on a misty fall morning while doves cooed in the trees and sparrows hopped about on the open space at the river's edge? She encountered a middle-age woman dressed in neon-pink tights who carried bright yellow weights in both hands and wildly swung them, oblivious to others passing by. She'd seen a couple of near misses when an especially quiet runner tried to pass her. You would think that people would be aware of others on the paths. The new loop might be a more solitary run or at least with a polite group of early morning joggers.

The day seemed a new adventure to Alice as she turned off her usual circuit and took the path through the park she recently found on an old city map. The fact she discovered the map was an unusual occurrence. While cleaning she found the map stuck on the top shelf of the closet in her small bedroom. The map had been published about fifty years ago, an illustrated reprint of a much older map of the park dating from the early 1920s. No one takes time for illustrated maps in today's digital world.

Peeling the map off the slightly sticky shelf, she thought it a stroke of good luck when she saw the beautifully drawn low stone walls, decorative larger arches, and a pagoda-like structure atop a small rise close to the river. Maybe the old structure would still be there and that would be her turn-around point.

Alice cut off at the loop she remembered from the map and after a few minutes of strenuous jogging she saw the pagoda in the distance. She slowed her pace and noticed the features of the area. The stone walls were placed randomly along the sides of the path. They were covered with leafy green vines and soft mosses. The fine gravel crunched pleasantly beneath her steps. With the absence of other people, the park's atmosphere felt pleasantly calm. She felt the stress slowly loosening its grip on her.

Across the path from the old pagoda, an elderly woman sat on a bench. As Alice slowly jogged by, she wondered about her. The woman dressed in what current fashion magazines call “vintage” clothing. Her posture prim yet her demeanor welcoming. A small perky dark purple hat sat pinned on top of a pile of white curls. A bright purple and pink scarf knotted around her neck called attention to her wrinkled face. A pale lavender jacket fit her wispy thin body nicely and was as faded as the black skirt that fell to her ankles. On her surprisingly dainty feet were sturdy brown lace-up shoes, the type seen in used clothing stores or old European films. On the ground beside the bench lay an upturned grey umbrella. Yellow and red dry leaves fluttered around the woman's feet and a few rested inside the open umbrella.

The bench where the old woman sat looked different from others in the main park. They were utilitarian, sturdy, pieces of metal. Some sported faded graffiti and were most often used by dog walkers who stopped for a rest or students as they consumed a bagel and drank coffee while they stared at their cell phones. This bench appeared ancient with an elaborately curved back of black iron, scrolled designs on the sides and dark wooden slats on the seat. Alice surmised the bench had been placed there long ago. Speculations churned within her mind. *It might be from early 20th century. Maybe donated from formal gardens of a dead philanthropist?* The woman on the bench smiled gently as she passed.

Alice slowed her pace as she came closer to the pagoda, her planned turn around point. The pagoda shimmered in the morning sun as the dew on its battered metal roof glistened with a silver haze. Still breathing hard from her run, Alice walked across the grass for a better look. The structure's design came from another time, another period that favored graceful lines and romantic patterns. Two sides had lovely circular designs in the shingles. An opening at the front looked like a giant inverted teardrop. Small wooden triangle shingles adorned the top third of the small building. Even with peeling white paint on the exterior, the overall effect was of an inviting children's play house. She ducked inside and gasped in wonder at the ceiling painted in shades of blue. Sprinkled among the blues were very detailed and realistic cream-colored clouds. She had never seen such a beautiful hand-painted ceiling.

Alice tried to think of an explanation. *How did the artist accomplish such a unique technique? Why was the pagoda in a forgotten part of the park when it should have been in a museum?*

Emerging from the delightful interior, Alice looked down the path toward the bench where the old woman sat. Perhaps she would know the story of the fading treasure of fanciful architecture. Alice walked briskly to the iron bench.

"Good morning. Lovely day." Alice spoke in a tentative voice to the stranger.

The woman nodded and then asked, "Is this your

first time to see the old pagoda?"

"Yes. I am really taken with it. Do you know anything about its origin? Why is it here?" Alice could not believe she actually spoke to a perfect stranger in a park as her reserved nature usually prevented her from such contact.

"I can tell you about the pagoda. However, not today. But I'll tell you about a unicorn." The woman spoke with an old-fashioned European accent that Alice had only heard once or twice. She couldn't remember where. The woman sounded like someone's grandmother from the old country.

"Please sit by me for a little while and relax. You look very tired for so early in the morning. Did you not sleep well, my dear?"

Alice had never been called "my dear" by anyone. *Who was this woman and why did she feel so compelled to talk with her?* She heard herself saying, "I would like very much to sit." She didn't remark on what the woman said about a unicorn, thinking she probably misheard the comment when trying to place her accent.

"My name is Arella, which means Angel in English. I prefer being called Angel. This bench is my place. I sit here and watch the day unfold. I'll tell you my story, if you have the time." Angel looked down and gently brushed away several dead leaves that drifted into the umbrella's open canopy.

Angel did not ask Alice's name. Alice felt that she did not need to tell Angel her name. Angel seemed to know her. Angel began her story with no further introduction or explanation.

2

DAY ONE—THE STORY OF THE UNICORN ANGEL

Once upon a time is the way stories always start but I will start by saying this: I believe in unicorns. You may tell me that a unicorn is a mythical creature appearing in old tapestries made back in the Middle Ages and talked about in romantic novels. However, I actually saw a unicorn. Yes, that's what I said. I did see a unicorn. Shall I continue or do you want to stop right now? You may go on your way unenlightened about the possibility of the existence of unicorns. Let me begin to tell what happened

My younger brother and I lived with our parents in a cottage in the old country. Oh, you don't need to know what country. Why do you think that important? We were always trying to escape doing chores around the cottage. Yes, that's right, I lived in a cottage in my youth. Cottages back then were nothing like today or the type you see at the cinema. Old cottages had leaky roofs and were known for chinks in the rock walls that let in light and cold air. Once a month I went to the river and hauled back a few good stones so Father could make repairs. You interrupt again? Oh, yes, the unicorn story. The unicorn had nothing to do with our cottage. May I proceed with the story? Are you sure you want to know about why I believe in unicorns? I will continue. One fair day I decided to take my brother with me on a new path through the woods to the spot where I usually collected the stones. We each carried a small bucket for the stones. Tangled branches and hanging moss overhung the path to the woods from our cottage. No, no, not Spanish moss, the kind of moss found there. Spanish moss is found somewhere south of here and I have never seen it. Enough questions about moss, my dear. Along the way, my brother complained of being tired and changed his mind about collecting stones with me that day. He said it was my assigned chore, not his, and refused to continue on our walk. He wanted to return to the cottage and help our father do other chores until time to repair the cottage walls. His behavior that day affirmed his laziness and his ability to shirk hard work every chance he got. He knew he could leave me there in the woods and I would carry on with my task. He turned back down the path towards home and I continued.

Somehow I missed the path that ran to the river and went unsuspectingly on my way deeper into the woods. Rounding a sharp bend in the path, I saw a large cave. Around the opening of the cave were very delicate tracks imprinted in soft mud. Being a curious child, I wanted to explore. The moment I walked into the cave's entrance, I felt a strange sleepiness come over me. Yes, yes, just like in the fairy tales, but this is about a unicorn, remember? I have found that interruptions of my story get me off track, so please no more questions. I will tell you about knowing there are things we don't understand and things that happen for which there is no realistic explanation. That's what unicorns really symbolize, though the old books won't tell you the truth about the matter.

I lay on the ground in the back of the cave and fell asleep for who knows how long. When I woke up, gradually like a child always does, I heard strange noises coming from beyond the woods in the direction of our cottage. Our cottage sat on the outskirts of the small village where others like my family lived. The noises were very loud and sharp sounds, repeated over and over for quite a sustained time. When I started to run out of the cave toward the path leading back to our cottage, a very strange thing happened. I felt caught up in a fantastic dream. A white horse with a brilliant coat of white mixed with silver streaks blocked the path back to my home. I saw the horse's rump first, but then it turned its head toward me. Amazed at what I saw, a beautiful curved golden horn came out of the front of its head. Though my parents raised me not to be superstitious, I first thought some magic spell had come upon me. As the creature turned toward me with the gleaming horn catching the filtered light from the woods, I realized the creature wanted to protect me from an unforeseen and horrible situation. When I reached to touch the shining silvery white coat or tried to walk past, it turned in such a way to keep me from the path back to our cottage. With a flash of intuition, I knew the truth of the situation. I knew I would never see my parents, my brother, or any of my friends again. A terrible evil force came and took them all away with the loud resounding sounds that reverberated through the woods. I will never forget those sounds, the sounds of many rifles.

I did not understand for many years what happened except that my family had been killed. All were shot for being who they were, poor villagers who practiced a religion not looked upon favorably by powerful people. The government allowed bands of angry soldiers to cleanse the land of others who did not adhere to officially government sanctioned beliefs and practices. My world changed in the time I slept in the cave. The unicorn protected me. I learned there are events in life that cannot be fully understood. Life continued for me in another way, another form, another time. Later in the refugee camps, kind villagers who found me in the cave helped me start a new life. So that is why I believe in unicorns. One saved me. It saved my life so my family line would go on when other families vanished that day.

**

"Did you like my story? Perhaps you can think about it and ask yourself if you will understand when you see a unicorn. You should be returning to your exercise routine. Perhaps we will meet again?"

The storyteller adjusted her little purple hat and

then bent to close the umbrella after emptying out stray leaves that accumulated during the story telling. She looked up expectantly at Alice and said, "You may leave now. Story is complete. Think about it, my dear. What does such a story mean in your life?"

Alice began to walk slowly away from the park bench. *Had she just heard a story about a unicorn and a very troubling attack that resulted in the loss of a child's family? A disturbing story from a total stranger!* Thoughts spinning, she found herself back on the paved path and gaining speed to her steps. She ran a sprint back to the apartment building two blocks away. The story of the unicorn returned to her thoughts the rest of the day as she went through the tedious hours of her courses. She listlessly took notes as the professors droned on and on, while she thought of her longing to return to the park and of her hope the strange storyteller would be there another day.

3

DAY ONE—MONDAY

BEA

The morning brought a series of minor annoyances for Bea. But then, Bea thrived on minor annoyances. First, hot water barely came out of the kitchen faucet indicating low pressure. Later Sweetie, her mixed breed dog, had an accident in the hallway and whined pitifully for fifteen minutes after she scolded him. Lastly, she misplaced Sweetie's leash and spent several minutes rummaging through the box of dog toys until she found it. Almost time to leave for the walk and she hadn't yet tied ribbons on her multiple braids. She had forgotten when she decided to put pink and red ribbons on her braids every day but it had become habit. After retirement from her job at the City Tax Office, she vowed she would wear her thick grey hair to suit herself. She had always wanted to wear braids. For years she kept the unruly natural locks trimmed very close to her scalp for a professional look. The supervisor had insisted employees look professional while collecting payments from people who straggled in during the early days of the month. Later, there were hordes of taxpayers who put off paying until the last days before deadlines. Her view of people, in general, soured during all those years of such work. All her fellow employees thought of Bea as the grumpiest woman alive and she enjoyed hearing them say it.

The dull tedium she experienced at work was not relieved by a happy family life. Bea's two daughters, Florence and Emmalou, who lived out West, hardly ever phoned. They certainly never sent her money to visit. The pension she earned barely got her by, but she learned to be content with her finances. She relied only on herself. That no-good husband of hers, Clarence, left fifteen years ago. Last year he had the nerve to try to reconcile with her when the doctor gave him a diagnosis of lung cancer after all those years of being a chain-smoker. The fancy lady, as Bea called the exotic dancer he ran off with, kicked him out of her place once she found out about his illness. Someone else would have to take care of Clarence, not Bea. She only took of care Bea.

Wearing bright colored housedresses from clearance racks in used clothing stores became her other small rebellion after years of imposed work dress codes. The dresses did not brighten her overall mood, but were worn for complete comfort. Three or four dresses usually lasted through multiple washings over several months of continuous use. Then she would tear them up for rags to be used for cleaning. Once she had the idea she would make a quilt of her old dresses, but soon gave up the idea since she did not have the patience to hand stitch. Besides, it would be too hard to stitch and watch her favorite soaps at the same time. The shows were her daily activity that filled the time during her long solitary afternoons.

Once retired, she found one individual who would drink coffee with her on a regular basis. She didn't think of the other woman as a friend, but as her neighbor who lived down the hall. The older black woman named Mamie lived alone in spite of her partial blindness and managed quite well. They met once a week on Fridays to discuss the progress of their soaps and complain about the noise the younger residents made at inconvenient hours.

Lately, she worried about her own expanding ample size. Previously, she justified the weight gain since retirement as a normal adjustment. Since no one cared what she did, she tried to stop thinking about the problem. Her constant companion Sweetie often made Bea more irritable when he whined or jumped on her sofa. Still, she kept to her daily routine. Her one regular weekly outing occurred on Monday evening when she played bingo at St. John's Catholic Church.

As Bea and Sweetie left the building, she stopped at the hall mailboxes to see if her Social Security check had arrived. It usually came on the first Monday of the month, but occasionally the check arrived on Tuesday. When she looked at the row of mailboxes she noticed a folded paper tucked in the top of her box. Funny, she never noticed it before today. Slightly yellowed with age, it was an illustrated map of the nearby park that had been published years ago. Pulling out the double folded map she looked at it with interest. She walked the park daily for many years, but had never seen details this old map revealed. At the far end of the park, a loop path led to a small structure overlooking the river.

"We are taking a new route today, Sweetie. My

feet will be okay. Maybe there won't be so many squirrels on this path." Bea used a voice that sounded like a mother talking to a baby when she spoke to Sweetie.

Once Bea and Sweetie came to the park's main paved path, Bea thought of the old map in her side pocket. *Yes, a new route would be nice. Maybe not as many other dog walkers.* She intensely disliked dog walkers with four or five dogs that strained on their leashes and barked at those who passed by. *Why would people spend money to have a dog walked?*

Soon she came to the loop shown on the old map and she stepped onto a fine gravel path. She had not previously noticed this path that wound closer to the river. In the distance she saw the dark outline of a small building, just like the map had shown. Her feet ached slightly and her breath became labored as she continued up the inclined path past some low stone walls covered in vines. Sweetie sniffed the sides of the path with obvious interest. Bea grew impatient. She saw a park bench ahead that would be a good place to sit and rest her feet. She would give Sweetie a treat or two and a little sip of water from the small bottle she carried in her tote. Sweetie started up with soft whines when Bea came closer to the bench. She saw someone sat there in the sunlight. She noticed the old structure that stood across the path closer to the river. It looked like some strange shaped fancy building in old parks during her grandmother's life, the type reserved for whites only. Not a good student of architecture, she thought it looked like a Chinese building. *What's the right word—pagoda?* She didn't want to walk as far as the building, but wanted to stop at the bench even if occupied by a stranger. *Maybe the person would move on and let her sit there alone. Some people don't like dogs.*

The woman who sat on the bench was dressed in all white with a loosely fitting cotton blouse and white embroidered skirt. Several bags of bread were at her feet and a few fat shiny pigeons pecked at the crumbs she threw on the other side of the path towards the river. The woman's large girth made Bea feel comfortable. Bea distrusted women who were too thin. She wouldn't mind if she had to share the bench for a moment's rest.

As she walked closer, Bea appraised the woman's appearance. Dark coarse hair streaked with grey peeked from under a big brimmed white straw hat, its band adorned with a single small dark purple artificial flower cluster. A jarring touch to the woman's all white dress were bright red tennis shoes with white laces. The shoes looked brand new. Bea approached rather warily as she pulled Sweetie away from the area where the pigeons waddled around and pecked at crumbs. The woman smiled at her cheerfully and gestured for her to sit at the other end of the bench. Her welcoming manner took Bea aback. She noticed the woman's light coffee colored face had no frown wrinkles and her dark black eyes glowed with warmth.

"You look like you need a sit down. Welcome." The friendly woman spoke with a slight Hispanic accent, not too noticeable, yet a trace lingered.

As she sat down, Bea saw the park bench looked very old. The black iron back curved at a pleasing angle and fancy whorls of iron decorated the sides. The smooth wooden planks of the bench were darkened from many years outdoors. Other benches she passed in the park looked nothing like this unusual one. Most were ordinary metal, no fancy designs, no feel of substance, just simple plain benches for public use.

A sudden flash of light caught in the corner of Bea's eye made her look toward the small building. The sun struck the metal roof and reflected a bright spot of light across the path. As she put her hand up to shield her eyes, the woman said, "You should look at the pagoda. It's very lovely antique. My name is

Bounty. I have lived in this country for long time. I still have back home in my voice."

Bea felt rather annoyed when the woman spoke to her in such a warm manner. She felt uncomfortable interacting with a stranger on a park bench. She did not really care to see an old building called a pagoda. She could care less where the woman lived. Bea only wanted to take a short rest before she turned back so she would be home in time for her routine of afternoon soaps.

"I think you can see pagoda another day," said Bounty as if reading Bea's thoughts. "You need a short story while you and your small pet rest here. I won't take too long to tell you a story about what my mamá saw in the jungle. You will like my story."

Bounty plunged right in with the storytelling before Bea could utter a word of protest.

4

DAY ONE—THE STORY OF THE UNICORN BOUNTY

My mamá believed in unicorns. Yes, the kind you read about in fairy tales. Well, other countries have such tales about unicorns. The Spanish word is *unicornio*. Much the the same, no? My mamá and her family lived in the backcountry far from the large cities. The nearest town was by the sea several miles away. Most people lived on small farms close to the jungles where they could farm off the land. Her parent's farmhouse and land adjoined the family farm of her grandfather. All of family shared the land and worked together to harvest nuts and fruits from the jungle. They also grew beans and corn on cleared family plots. My mamá, Blanca, was admired for her lovely cream colored skin. Well, those things show up in families as you must know. She worked like all the other small children to pick the wild fruit that grew close to a nearby spring. The family used all the good jungle plants for food, medicines, and trade with other families who did not have the same things growing on their land.

She asked her older brother to go with her that day. Oh yes, there were several children, not sure how many. Large families meant many workers. Her brother wanted to rest from his chores of helping their papá clear a new garden, so he agreed to walk with her to the spring that day. Actually, her brother was slightly lazy—she told me many years later—and wanted to quit being a farmer like their papá. He wanted to find some of his friends who had left to join a group that had something to do with the government. My mamá did not remember too many of the details about that, but she did remember what happened when she saw the unicorn. Well, yes, I did say a unicorn like the fairy tales. Well, yes, it did look like pictures in the old children's books. Yes, a unicorn, *mi amiga! Si, si,* a small deer animal, well, maybe a small horse is what she said, with a horn sticking up in the middle of the head. You made me go back to my language with all your questions.

Please let me tell you the story like she told me.

My mother ran up the trail ahead of her brother and discovered a small path that looked like a shorter way to the springs where the fruits grew. After she took the turn she realized that her brother was not behind her, but she thought he would catch up. The jungle grew darker along the path until she saw a small clearing ahead. At the side of the clearing where the land started to rise toward the mountains, she saw a small opening in the hill covered with branches and fallen small trees. Thinking she would only peek inside, she said she felt drawn into the strange little cave against her will and became very sleepy as she entered. Her memory about many things left her in later years, but she declared with much certainty that part of the story. She believed a kind spirit in the cave gathered her in and kept her there until she fell asleep. No, she wasn't *loca!* Let me finish and then you will understand.

When she woke up she saw a beautiful creature standing in the clearing outside the cave of branches. Dreaming or taken by strange visions, she did not know what had happened or why the creature stood before her. In the distance, sounding through the treetops, she heard loud shouts and many *pistola* shots. She knew the sound of *una pistola* because once her papá shot a young jaguar that wandered into the garden. The unicorn stood in the clearing and scared my poor mamá out of her wits. The size of the forest deer but with a brilliant white coat, the animal's golden horn on its head gleamed in the sunlight of the clearing. She said she would never forget its large black eyes shining in fierce protection. Suddenly, my mamá understood that the creature intended to keep her from crossing the clearing back to the path home. She called for her brother over and over but the unicorn pranced, stamped its small black hooves, and blocked her way. She became so frightened she stayed in the cave. Her brother never came. The sound of shots stopped. The silence of the jungle terrified her even more.

My mamá swore by the blessed Virgin that she had been protected that day by the lovely animal from the terrible fate of her parents and brother. They had been killed by armed men who came to the farm and demanded all of the family's food.

My mamá watched as the beautiful animal ran away into the shadows of the dense tree and she heard heavy footsteps running up the path to the clearing. There appeared in the clearing a group of two women, three small children, and one old man who were all hysterical with terror of what had happened. None of them were her family. They gathered her up and all of them walked for many miles to the town by the sea. They reported the raid by the terrible armed men. The same men would later destroy her country's peace. There were many years of struggle and horrible things happened to other innocent farmers. She knew she had survived, been protected by something, some visitation she could not understand. She went to new life in another country. Her life's purpose was to continue our family line. She learned a new language but she always told her stories in the old tongue. Did she dream this? Hmmmm....is that what my story told you? Whether Mamá had a vision or a dream, she believed a beautiful creature with a golden horn saved her life for a reason. She said it happened to her. I believed her story and so did many others who heard her tell it.

Now, what did you think of the story? Perhaps you can think about it. Ask yourself if you will understand when something fantastic happens to you. You never had anything fantastic happen in all your life? It's not too late. Perhaps you will see a unicorn. Life can change and turn out better than you imagined. Maybe learning that will make you happy.

**

Bea rose quickly from the bench and stumbled over the bags of bread Bounty had placed on the ground. Sweetie tugged at the leash. “Oh, so sorry. Your story was...how to say this...rather different. Not sure what you meant. I guess I should say thanks for sharing the bench. I need to get home.”

“Maybe we will meet again in the park,” Bounty said in a happy tone. “I like telling stories. I hope you will understand about the unicorn.”

As Bea walked slowly home she thought about the strange woman and her story. *In what country did that woman Bounty say her mother lived? Wonder what country my ancestors came from? I know they didn’t escape from their homes. They were brought as slaves across the ocean. But don’t know how it happened. Mmmmm...unicorns and my family. Why didn’t a unicorn save them?*

5

DAY ONE – MONDAY

CAROL

At three o'clock the last bell rang signaling the end of another school day at P.S. 236. The school was located one block from the park across the street from the aging apartment building where Carol lived. She worried it would not be her home much longer. Carol's mom had a good job at the law office, but now with her dad gone bills weren't being paid on time.

She volunteered to help the teacher tidy up the room after the bell rang. Soft loose brown curls fell into her eyes as she bent over to pick up torn papers dropped by careless students. She put boxes of supplies back in the cabinets and reshelved the reading group books. She wanted to feel needed by her teacher. As she heaved the faded red backpack up on her thin shoulders, Carol exited from the classroom more slowly this particular Monday. Her two friends, Kathy and Celeste, were going to the after-school program. She enjoyed the various activities which included art, reading, beading crafts or board games. All the kids, including Carol and her friends, loved outdoor game time that took place on the concrete pad recreation area. This was the first month she couldn't go with the only two friends she had made at school. Seventh grade can be a hard place to make friends and she would miss the fun times with them after school. For the first time this school year, her mom couldn't afford the monthly fee and her instructions had been to go straight home after school.

One of the few light brown skinned children in her class, Carol often felt out of place. Her lovely, but sad dark eyes gave a luminous look to her small heart shaped face. She inherited her mom's East Indian features and none of her auburn- haired Irish dad's physical traits. A strapping big man and former Army sergeant, her dad had been best suited for a career in the military and not for civilian life. Civilian life gave him too many choices and he made many bad ones.

Since the trip to India with her mother last summer, things changed for Carol. She knew her grandparents who died in a terrible train crash only from faded photographs that were a part of the home altar for as long as she could remember. The unfamiliar rituals of a Hindu funeral, swarms of solemn cousins who lived in the small village, the large cities they traveled through on dirty trains were all a blur to Carol. She never wanted to go to India again or acknowledge her family ties to such a horrible, crowded place. Carol shocked her mom when she angrily stated that since she lived in America, she would live as an American. She packed away all of her pastel colored saris that she wore when the family dressed for dinners with other Indian families. Since their return to the States and her dad's departure, there had been no contact with any of them due to her mom's shame as an abandoned woman with a child to support.

Carol could not procrastinate leaving school any longer. Recently she discovered the nearby park with great places to sit and read, to draw in her sketch pad, or to sit and watch boats on the river. She especially liked to see the sail boats with the two or three people who sat in the bows as they glided by. The larger tugs were squatty and ugly but she rated them as her second favorite. Her teacher assigned her a project on tugboats two weeks ago. She learned about them from books in the public library. In one of the books she checked out, she found a folded map that looked quite old. Upon examining it more closely she recognized the park close to her apartment. The paper, slightly yellowed, felt thin between her fingers. Most of the places in the park were marked distinctly, all except one. The map showed a loop off the main path toward the river. She determined to walk until she found the faintly marked path and a small building shown close to the river. She hoped for a pretty place she could spend time each afternoon. Maybe she would see a tugboat and could copy its colors for an illustration in her report.

Carol walked slowly to the park as she knew she could spend about two hours there. Often her mom returned home by 5:30, but Carol didn't want to be in the apartment alone, especially now with her dad gone. In the past, he made snacks and encouraged her to do her homework. His drinking never started until after dinnertime and by then she could shut herself in her own room and wear headphones to listen to music that blocked out her parents' arguments. She feared if she and her mom moved out of the two bedroom apartment, she would have to share a bedroom with her mom and that would be a terrible idea—terrible in that she loved her alone time in her own bedroom.

After walking her usual route up the main path of the park she remembered the map and looked toward the river for the other small path. *It was there all right!* The path veered gently off toward the river and its fine gravel that made a nice crunchy sound as she walked past the low stone walls covered with vines and flowers. In the distance something glowed in the afternoon light that reflected from the river—a small building that looked like a fancy playhouse.

A teenager sat on a bench across from the structure. Warned about talking to strangers, Carol put her head down and hurried past the girl, pretending to be intent on her walk. When Carol turned to take a fast look over her shoulder, she saw the girl played with a deck of cards not paying any attention to her. Eager to take a closer look at the fancy little house, she quickened her steps. She briefly glanced back again at the bench and noticed the bench looked pretty fancy, too. *It would be a great thing to draw with the swirly lines and curlicue back. That looks like a really old design. Yes, what an amazing place!* Her brain filled with ideas of drawings that would be great for her sixth period art class. Her teacher encouraged students to look around for interesting objects to draw and she found two objects today—the old playhouse up ahead and a fancy park bench. Surely no one else in the class would think of drawing these unusual things. Most of her classmates drew in the new Japanese comic book style, but she longed to be more a serious artist. The teacher would certainly praise her for submitting drawings different from everyone else.

The small funny building looked very old the closer she got to it. She stepped off the path and crossed the grass up the slightly rising terrain. The outside of the small building had old white peeling paint and patches of light brown stains. It made Carol sad to see such a ruined place. Two sides had large circles cut out of the walls. She wondered about the unusual tear-drop shaped opening that led inside. When she entered, she noticed a rather musty old smell and wanted to hold her nose. Carol looked up at the ceiling and saw an amazing sight she hadn't expected. The ceiling was painted several shades of blue that blended into each other like a real sky. Clouds that looked like real clouds were scattered among the blues. It reminded Carol of a water coloring technique she tried in art class. The ceiling looked realistic but also hazy. She wondered how the painter did it. She would definitely ask her art teacher Miss Brandt.

Several minutes later Carol stepped out after admiring the beautiful blue ceiling, and to her surprise, the girl still sat on the bench across the path. The teenager's casual manner was like other teenagers encountered in the mall when she and her mother shopped for school uniforms. The older girls acted cool but bored. The slender teen dressed in all black fashionably cut sports clothing. Long straight black braids hung from under a grey cap with a dark purple brim. Carol glimpsed silver colored slippers on the teen's petite feet. She noticed the girl's features seemed a mixture just like her. Biracial is what her teacher called kids with parents of different races. Carol's East Indian and Irish heritage was uncommon—maybe the girl on the bench was another mixture no one would easily guess. She didn't look scary like someone Carol shouldn't approach and ask a question. Maybe, the girl would know about the little building. Pretending to be braver than she actually felt, Carol walked up to the girl in black on the bench.

"Excuse me, please. Oh, my name is Carol. Do you know the name of the little fancy playhouse across the path?" Carol couldn't believe she had spoken to a stranger, but she prided herself in being polite.

"Hi kid. I'm Charity. Yeah, it's a pagoda. Sort of a Far East thing, well, maybe mostly Chinese like me."

"Do you come here a lot?" Carol smiled to think she had been right about the girl's mixed race.

"I've been around some. What are you doing in this part of the park? Does your mom know you're here?"

"Hey, I am not a kid. Bet I am close to your age."

"No, probably not. I'm older than I look—it's the Chinese influence. We all look alike right?"

"Funny you saying that. Are you mixed like me?"

"Mixed? Oh, you mean are we both bi-racial? I have heard that before, too. Makes you feel weird, right?'

"Yeah, guess so."

"Well, I can tell you a story that you would probably think is weird. Do you want to hear it?"

"A story that's weird? You want to tell me a story like I am some little kid? Well, I've got stuff to do at home."

"No, wait, Carol, I didn't mean to sound like a jerk. I really have a story to tell you. Come on, you don't want to go home and be all alone, right?"

Carol gulped. "How did you know I would be alone at home?

Obvious. Why else would you hang out in the park?" Charity smiled.

Against all rules that her mother taught her, Carol sat down on the odd old park bench next to a very smart talking teenager she just met and tried to look ready to hear a story.

Charity spoke in a calm voice as she began the story. The cards in her hands still fluttered softly in a continuous soft shuffle.

6

DAY ONE—THE STORY OF THE UNICORN CHARITY

Once upon a time...no, just joking, OK? Well, you may not really believe this story but my grandmother told it to me. She is really, really old and never, ever lies to anyone. In fact, she tells the truth too much is what I think. Anyway, this happened to her when she was young girl, you know, kind of like you, barely in her teens. OK, OK, I know you are not a kid, just messing with you. Seriously, this story has implications. You got that word, right?

My grandmother lived in a small village in a far-away land. Yeah, China. Good guess. All of her family lived there. When a girl got married she went to live with her husband's parents which fulfilled the long-standing custom of the people. As a new daughter-in-law they treated her like a slave for a long time until her grown-up son got married. Then she treated her new daughter-in-law like a slave and so on.

Anyway, my grandmother was daughter number one, and it's really bad if you are the firstborn girl. Yeah, it really sucks. Back then, maybe even still, the families wanted a boy first. Something about always taking care of the parents and carrying on the family name. There were other sibs, but she was the oldest. One of her younger brothers had died from something really bad. The family then worried that there was only one boy left and the other three were girls. Oh yeah, and just to let you know, these people did not go to school very much, especially girls. All the girls had to work, work, work and have babies when they were old enough. OK, enough family history and culture, right?

Well, my grandmother saw a unicorn one day that changed her life. Have you ever seen those old paintings, I guess they are actually ink drawings or something, from China and really weird animals are in them? The fish look strange with big eyes. Some of the birds look huge, but in other pictures they are just little tiny strokes that represent birds. You will learn all of that the more art you study. How did I know about your art? Hey, you just look like you're artsy. I'm telling you the truth. I'm going on with the story now. My grandmother really saw a live unicorn! Yeah, yeah, that kind of nonexistent animal, a unicorn. The fairy tales call it a mythical creature, something like a little horse. People probably thought they saw it running through the woods or they were crazy or something and then started drawing what they remembered they thought they saw. Yeah, they called it a unicorn because it has one large horn coming out of its forehead. Sure, I have seen some pictures in European art books that look like it is coming out of the top of the head, but I guess in the Far Eastern part of the world, those crazy people who thought they saw one said it came out of its forehead. Yeah, they were white little horses over there, too. So enough with the interruptions, let me tell you the freaking story. Sorry, not a good word to use. Right. Don't use that word, OK?

Charity continued the story and Carol kept quiet.

My grandmother had a lot of work to do every day as the oldest daughter. Her duties included airing out the beds and rolling them up for the day—people actually slept on mats on the floors of their houses, kind of like camping out in sleeping bags, I guess. She fed the chickens and the two pigs in the yard behind the house. I would think having pigs right next to the house made it very stinky but that's where she said they lived. Her mother started cooking for the day early in the morning and she helped with the preparation, too. Her father wanted wild onions in the stews and rice dishes made by her mother—must have been a lot of rice. One of her main chores each day was to pick fresh onions for the family to use. When she first began the chore, her old uncle would walk with her to the nearby springs a little ways into the forest and show her how to find the onions her father liked so well. She remembered hearing lots of stories from him when they went on these walks. As an old man, Uncle could not contribute much to the family, being partially blind and too weak to cut wood. She remembered when he could see everything around him. Her father said Uncle's eyes got cloudy like all old men's eyes do. He could see well enough to walk up the path into the woods with her. From an early age, Uncle memorized every plant in the forest. He would ask her to pick a certain leafy pale green plant near an old tree and once she brought it to him, he would smell, feel, and even bite into the plant. He would tell the name of the plant and its use. Of course, even as a younger girl she knew what the onions looked like and how they smelled. She learned that the onions grew mostly in a sunny spot close to the little springs. The bright glossy green of the onion stems were easily seen among the other plants growing nearby. What? Oh yeah, I got off the real story there didn't I? I promised to tell you about the unicorn.

So...the day she saw the unicorn her uncle insisted she take her younger brother with her to gather onions. By now she knew exactly where the stand of onions grew by the springs. Uncle instructed her to show Younger Brother the plants and teach him their uses. He told her that knowledge must be passed on in the family. She thought he favored Younger Brother and that she would not be trusted as a girl to keep the knowledge. The two children left the village and walked into the forest and up the path towards the springs. Her mother asked her to hurry home that day as she worried that something terrible might happen soon. Her mother often talked like that to the children, but Grandmother always thought she meant to scare the children into being quiet and obedient. The villagers had seen planes flying low in the skies for the last two days. A traveling company of traders stopped by the village a few weeks earlier and told stories of how the country was in danger from being invaded by their enemies. Grandmother did not know much about talk of enemies, but her parents gathered up food and hid it in various places like in the old chicken coop and in the rafters of the house. When she asked about the enemies, her mother told that they were foreign devils and might come and take all their food and capture the young women of the village. She thought that enemies must need someone to do all their chores if they wanted the women.

Younger Brother did not want to walk to the springs. He complained he hated onions. She knew that Father would be very angry if there were no onions for dinner. After the two argued about how onions smelled up the kitchen and as she tried to pull him along with her on the path, Younger Brother ran away down the path and back towards the village. Always the obedient child, she continued on her way to pick the onions. As she rounded the curve in the path she noticed that some larger boulders had recently fallen from one side of the hill where the spring flowed. A very small dark cave had been opened in the side of the hill.

Being a curious girl, she stepped into the darkened opening and had a strange sensation of apprehension. Overcome with dizziness, she collapsed to the ground and fell into a dreaming state. After who knows how long, she roused to the sound of distant mechanical noises. What she heard frightened her so much she began to tremble.

A moving shadow appeared in front of the cave. At first she thought one of the small deer that lived in the hills had come to browse in the clearing. The animal stood a few feet outside the cave and stood alert, listening to the strange sounds echoing through the forest. When she tried to walk out of the cave, the creature snorted and pawed the earth in front of the entrance. Its white coat glistened in the sun. Grandmother looked with astonishment at a marvelous feature on the animal—a beautiful golden horn. It shone in the sunlight and cast ripples of light across the meadow by the stream. A horn on a little horse? Yeah, yeah, the unicorn...that's how they always look. One large golden horn, white shining coat and smaller than a real pony. Yeah, I think it would be fun to ride like a pony, but what about that big horn?

So, let me finish up here. Grandmother also told me the unicorn flashed amazing silver hooves that sparkled like diamonds. I think she imagined that part. The unicorn would not let her out of the cave. She waited and waited for what seemed like a long time. She began to cry and begged the unicorn to let her pass out of the cave, but evidently unicorns don't understand Chinese. Ha-ha, get it?

Repeated gunfire broke the silence of the forest. The sounds reverberated into the hills. At last there came a stunning stillness like she had never experienced. She tried to run out of the cave, but the prancing unicorn blocked her way. At the sound of thudding footsteps coming up the path, the unicorn turned and looked at her one last time, pawed the ground with a dainty sparkling hoof, and ran into the forest. The gleam of the golden horn faded into the shadows.

Two people ran into the clearing. Old Aunt, her father's sister, and another young boy cousin staggered—breathless and terrified—to where she stood in the front of the cave. The three of them stayed for one night, huddled together from fear. The next morning after they gathered what plants they could find for food, the three walked for many miles until they reached the town in the valley. Old Aunt would not tell her what happened in the village, only that the foreign devils had stolen all the food and kidnapped young women. Her mother's predictions were fulfilled. My grandmother knew the unicorn saved her life that day.

Many months later, Old Aunt finally told her about the terrible day when she became an orphan. The whole family had been shot by the soldiers except for two girl cousins who were only thirteen and fourteen. From where Old Aunt hid in the rafters of their house, she saw them taken away on the trucks that brought the foreign devils into their village. I think horrible things happened to those two girls. Being saved by the unicorn meant that she would be the only one left to carry on the family name. After the wars were finally over and Grandmother came to this country, she married another refugee. She bore four children, my mother and her three brothers. Of course! They were all Americans! Now, I want you to think about what this all means. Yes, believing in unicorns and being saved by one is a very special experience, all right.

**

"You sure had lots of questions. Better head home, kid...uh, Carol. Sorry again about that. Your mom might not understand that you were late because you heard a unicorn story from a stranger. But, FYI, I'm not a stranger."

Carol left Charity at the bench and began to walk on the gravel path back to the main park. The fact that she had overcome her fear and actually talked to a stranger amazed her. A feeling she'd not experienced in several months—confidence—made her tingle with contentment. Yet, the story about the unicorn troubled her. Being saved by a unicorn, even if the story was made up, gave her something serious to think about. She wondered if she would ever be saved from a terrible disaster in her future.

7

DAY TWO—TUESDAY

ALICE

Alice woke up with a start. Oh God, Tuesday. So soon. She remembered her paper on the viability of through streets versus circular round-abouts in upscale neighborhoods due for afternoon class. She didn't want to spend the morning trying to improve it and then retyping the whole thing. She didn't want to think about up-scale neighborhoods. She dressed quickly in her running shorts and a long sleeve warm-up top. Today she chose a bright orange one after she looked out the bedroom window and saw a cloudy dreary day. Wearing something bright made her think of life, brightness, and nature. With a quick glance toward the bathroom mirror, she saw her same tired self. Pulling a stiff brush through her thick dark brown hair, she thought about her experience in the park yesterday. *What a strange old woman in the park. I asked a question about the pagoda, not about the need for a story. The old woman must have been confused about her strange story. Very odd to tell a story like that to someone who happened to pass by during the early morning. She said something about me accepting things I couldn't understand? Somehow that's connected to a unicorn? What could that possibly mean?* She walked down the short hallway from her door to the stairway leading to the ground floor.

Alice did her prerequisite warm-up stretches on the curb outside the front door of the building. As usual, Alice started with a brisk walk, then changed to a slow run. She rounded the corner into the park and dodged other joggers as she settled into an easy cross-country style stride. She'd participated in cross-country for two years in high school before she joined the school newspaper club as a writer. She had loved writing the assigned stories. Her dad had encouraged her by telling her that writing skills were an asset for any future job.

As she increased her pace she wondered if the woman named Angel would be in the park. Alice's heart raced with the expectation that she might see the old woman again and remembered the pleasant but unsettling experience of hearing a story told by the kind old lady. When she found herself at the end of her regular route, she didn't see the gravel path that led to the left toward the river. *How could she have missed it?* She started doing the jogging jig that young women do when trying to run in place to keep up their heart rate while killing time at a stop light. She circled back and looked for the path more carefully. Finally she saw the path, just past a plain aluminum park bench that looked sad and forsaken. A plain bench unlike the beautiful black iron bench she discovered yesterday. Dry brown leaves covered the seat. *Strange, she thought, modern parts of the park looked unfriendly and strictly utilitarian. The older area looked inviting and enchanted.* With anticipation she ran slightly faster until her foot hit a large stone. She slid precariously to the right and came down on her right ankle.

"Oh shit," she said aloud. She felt better when she cursed. The habit showed her rebellion against her mother's lectures about being a lady in all situations even when you injured your ankle in a large city park. She saw the black iron bench up ahead. Carefully, she pulled herself up on the stone wall. Another stone fell onto the path at her feet.

"Oh great, now the old park takes revenge by throwing stones at newcomers," she whispered.

Her deeply skinned ankle oozed blood. As she limped closer to the bench she noticed the roof of the pagoda across the path shone brilliant yellow. She saw a large bare aspen tree towering over the pagoda. It must have dropped its leaves overnight covering the roof. Other scattered golden leaves lay on the grass like small piles of shining jewels.

Yep, nature does provide moments of beauty, something a concrete and steel city will never do. Yep, I think I'm in the wrong major.

Angel, the storyteller, sat on the bench, wearing the same vintage clothing as the day before when they met. The grey umbrella lay upturned on the ground beside her brown sturdy shoes. It was as if she never left.

"Hello, Alice. My dear, what have you done to yourself? I heard you say something but couldn't hear what you said."

"Just talking to myself. You called me Alice. I don't think I introduced myself yesterday."

"I know you're Alice. Perhaps you should take care of that bleeding ankle now that introductions are done."

"It's really not anything to worry about. I'm a little

shaken. May I sit for a minute?"

"Of course, you may. Thank you for being so polite. I hope you have time to hear another story this morning while you rest and care for your injury. Here, take my handkerchief." Angel handed her a beautifully embroidered soft cotton cloth, its lace edging yellowed with age.

"No, no, I won't use that. It's too lovely and the blood will stain."

Alice reached into her jacket to retrieve a tissue and dabbed at the large oozing scrape on her ankle.

"I thought about your unicorn story. Will this one be as unbelievable?"

"My dear girl, believing is all about learning and learning is all about something else that I don't need to tell you right now. Doesn't matter except that you must remember stories are important." She spoke in a rush of words as if she'd lost patience with Alice.

Angel took a very deep breath for someone so wispy thin and began her story, her odd accent more distinct than Alice remembered.

8

DAY TWO—THE STORY OF A FLOOD ANGEL

I want to tell you about a flood, a sinister thing that either comes slowly and steadily or all at once in a mad fury at unsuspecting victims. I experienced a flood as a younger person. Yes, long time ago. I don't remember what year, so don't ask. Rude question. Try not to interrupt with such questions. I lived in between country after I lost my parents. Inbetween country, how to say, in between here and there. Shall I continue? The family I worked for allowed me to occupy a little room was attached to a large shed near the cow pen. The simple furnishings were a small bed, a rickety pine table, and a hard backed chair. The family paid me a few coins...wages, of course not dollars...well, they paid me something. Well-fed and a roof over my young head made my life easier than before. In the winter a little stove kept me warm. I loved that little stove since it reminded me of the cottage I grew up in. A little stove there, too, that must have been destroyed...well, you know what happened.

Early winter rains were prolonged that year. The heavy downpours prevented the men from the harvest. I did all the chores assigned inside the main house where the farmer and his wife lived but my other outdoor chores could not be performed. Paid by the hour? What an unusual question. A farm worker got paid in those days for work on the farm until no more work for the day. The steady unrelenting rain made me extremely sad. My friend Gretta said I still grieved over my losses, meaning my whole family. She said I needed to find a good man to marry and I could begin a new life. Gretta, the housemaid at the next farm over, lived inside the farmhouse with her employers. The prosperous farmer provided comfortable accommodations for his workers.

Did I mention that my little room was attached to a milking shed for the two cows that produced large quantities of milk? I made soft sweet smelling cheese and rich pale yellow butter to be sold at the market on Saturdays. My mother taught me to make cheese as soon as I could stand on a small stool and reach the wooden table where she worked. From eight years of age I milked the cows. I knew cows and how valuable they were to a family farm. And I loved cows, their lovely sad eyes, the way they quivered when one first touched them before starting the milking—so many nice things about cows. It is a shame that people no longer have any connection to useful and necessary animals that provide for them, don't you agree? I still miss those cows.

The day the flood rushed through the farmyard became a most unfortunate day for the cows. We penned them so they would not wander off and become trapped in muddy holes that were overflowing with the cold steady rain. I was the first one on the farm to hear the low rumbling sounds swelling from the direction of the stream that ran through the wood lot north of the farmhouse. I looked out the window and saw the flood of water rushing into the lower part of the farmyard where the cows were penned. Poor animals, they were helpless as the water swept them against the strong wooden log fence. I shook in horror as they thrashed back and forth against the fence as the water pulled them from their feet. My little room was not in the path of the furious water that killed the cows; yet, I trembled in terror as the waters rushed by and trapped me inside. As I watched the floating bodies of the two beloved cows my tears flowed until the water passed. Afterward, I ran through the muck and the debris of the flood to the farm house where the famer and his wife sat in the front window watching the floating cows. The farmer's wife cried and shouted at the farmer that the family would not survive until spring without the cows and money from sales of cheese and butter. The dead bodies of the cows lay in the mud of the flooded pen. The partially harvested barley fields were lost two weeks ago due to the steady rains. The potato fields were mired in deep mud. The ripe potatoes lay buried and would rot before the flood waters receded. The disasters multiplied the prospect of a harsh winter of hunger and deprivation.

I told the farmer and his wife that I would help with dead cows, but he asked me to first look into the milking shed to see what damage the flood caused. Despondent about the loss of his productive cows, he needed to purchase new cows before winter knowing they couldn't be milked until spring. Uncertain if he could secure a loan from the village money-lender, the farmer and the wife began shouting at each other in fury. I left the farmer and his wife arguing loudly and hurried to the outside yard.

Carefully, I crossed the thick mud close to the pens where the cows lay drowned and saw the door to the shed torn off from the torrent of water. Entering the milking room I could see where the water rushed in bringing small tree limbs, dead plants and other unidentifiable trash. A pile of sodden material lay at the threshold. Picking up the heavy broom from the back of the shed, I swept the pile out the door. I expected to find only wet trash but I saw a brown canvas bag, tied tightly with a small piece of rope. As I retrieved the bag from the soaked materials, it felt heavy and made a slight clinking sound. With difficulty I unknotted the thin rope and looked inside. Yes, yes, my dear, coins! Eight golden coins nestled inside the sodden bag. I found eight lovely antique coins from another time,

What I held in my hand would support the farm for several years. A found treasure brought by the flood from who knows where. Really, must you interrupt so much? The country's history overflowed with tales of gypsy traders, bandits, kings and such. Why shouldn't there be a treasure bag uncovered by a flood? I imagined the coins were stolen by robbers who once lived in the forest and buried them meaning to return one day. I made up stories in my mind about who might have owned the bag in another life. The bag of coins in my possession could change my life.

After I swept out the muddy leaves from the shed, I returned to my little room, sat on the bed and lit a candle. I sat there for a long time as I considered a reasonable plan. I withdrew four coins from the bag for myself. I hid the coins under a loose floor board, knowing I should take my time to consider how to take advantage of my small treasure. I'm not a dishonest person. I thought of my future. I carefully retied the thin rope around the neck of the bag and took the tattered bag with the four remaining coins to the farmer. He praised me effusively as an honest and faithful worker. I rejoiced with him and his happy wife that there would be enough money to buy one new cow and supplies for the coming winter. He would buy seeds to replant the barley and potatoes next spring. The money from the sale of the coins saved the farm. I foresaw a brighter future for myself. The flood washed away my grief, my sense of loss and despair gone. My heart sang with hope knowing I could begin a new life when the right time came. I would not forever remain a young orphaned milking maid with no prospects.

**

Angel stopped speaking abruptly and looked down at Alice's ankle.

"Oh, I see the bleeding stopped. Why are you looking at me so strangely?"

"Angel, you tell unusual stories but are they really about you? Unbelievable, the things you say happened."

"Just ponder, dear girl. Thoughts of what it all means will come to you. These lessons take time."

Angel reached for the umbrella on the ground which seemed to be a signal to Alice that she should leave the bench and continue on her way. Her ankle stopped hurting enough to walk fairly briskly down the path to go home. When she looked back over her shoulder, she could not see the gravel path turning off to the pagoda. How strange. I must have jogged farther than usual before my fall. She puzzled over Angel's last remarks as she came to the front steps of her building. The dreary task of completing the paper due for her afternoon class loomed before her.

9

DAY TWO—TUESDAY

BEA

As the light shone in the eastern window, Bea groaned and looked at the clock on the maple bed stand. The dial read nine o'clock. The alarm hadn't gone off. She forgot to set it and this annoyed her. Not an unfamiliar feeling for Bea, she felt annoyed or irritable most of the time. Noises from apartments above her, sounds of the trash trucks, occasional sirens on the street, barking dogs, loud music coming from open windows, all were annoyances to Bea. She heard Sweetie's paws thumping on the floor beside the bed and looked down to see a small puddle in the corner of the room. *Not again, Sweetie! You whined just a minute ago. Stupid of me not to get up then.*

After cleaning up Sweetie's mess with a paper towel and spraying a disinfectant over the area, she took Sweetie's leash and led him down the back stairs to the small yard at the back of the building for his usual morning doggie ritual.

Bea returned to the apartment for her breakfast. She and Sweetie watched the morning shows, the usual fare about how to get along with your in-laws or how to arrange a perfect brunch party for ten guests. None of those topics applied to Bea, but she liked to watch and pass the time until her noon-time walk in the park. When she took Sweetie outside earlier, the overcast sky looked threatening with grey clouds so she pulled on a light blue sweater over her flowered house dress. The fall weather had been unpredictable, but hopefully by noon it would only be cool with no drizzling mist. Dreary weather made Bea feel down in the dumps and even more grouchy.

Bea and Sweetie left the apartment at noon. As she crossed the street, she remembered her conversation yesterday with the cheerful woman on the park bench. *You never know what people will say.* Bea puzzled over the woman's tale about a unicorn that saved her mamá from a village massacre. She should have told her that she did not believe the foolish tale. The woman could be slightly crazy. Bea passed the gravel path that led to the left closer to the river and tried to deliberately walk on. However, Sweetie tugged at the leash in the direction of the gravel path and seemed interested in investigating smells around the low stone walls. Sweetie always did what he wanted on the daily walk, so Bea relented and turned three steps back. As she stepped onto the little path Sweetie strained the leash in the direction where Bea had met the talkative large woman on the black iron bench. If the woman who introduced herself as Bounty sat there today, Bea planned on walking past without speaking to her. *Why would anyone name a child Bounty? She looked Hispanic, probably changed it to try to be more American. She seems very odd.*

No one sat on the old fashioned bench as Bea walked by with Sweetie. *What a relief!* There were crusty bread crumbs scattered on the path but no pigeons in sight. The old small building loomed ahead on the left. Sweetie suddenly pulled the leash. Bea stumbled and dropped the leash as Sweetie ran toward the structure. *Bad dog, bad dog, come back here.* Bea huffed heavily as she tried to run after the dog. She hated to run and never did.

Sweetie's misbehavior made her very angry. Bea saw Sweetie run into the little building and his high pitched barks echoed inside. As Bea came closer, she remembered a recent documentary she watched about tourist spots in the Far East. The building looked like pagodas in the film, but badly needed repairs. The opening in the front had a strange shape, like a teardrop. Bea noticed circular windows were on two sides. *Odd, very odd.* She called for Sweetie to come out; but when the dog continued to bark, Bea stepped inside to retrieve her disobedient pet. She focused on grabbing the loose leash the dog dragged around the dirty floor in circles. *Bad dog, bad dog. Come here.* She took Sweetie's leash firmly in her hand. *Huh! This place is a terrible mess. Must have been some wasteful city project.* She worked for the city long enough to know there were many projects started but often not finished. If they were completed, they were not maintained. *Must have been what happened here—again—always does when the city is involved.*

As she emerged from the pagoda with Sweetie under control, she looked across the path and then groaned to herself. *Oh no, the woman in white on the bench!* She determined not to let the woman engage her in a long conversation today.

"*Hola, buenas dias!*" Bounty called to Bea as she approached the bench.

"You visited the pagoda! Did you like what you saw?"

"Humph," grunted Bea. "Just another run down city project. My dog made me chase him inside."

"Maybe another day you can take a better look and understand, OK? Are you ready to hear another story?"

"No, no. No time today for stories...unless you tell me a true life story, unlike the one about a unicorn. And I want you to know where your mamá lived."

Bounty's face reddened at Bea's implication that the unicorn story lacked veracity. She sighed heavily and completely ignored Bea's demand to tell where her mamá lived.

"You'll maybe understand better this story because it has chickens, not a unicorn. I start now or do you want feed the birds first? I stopped feeding them when you walked by on your way to the pagoda."

"You weren't sitting on the bench when I passed by!" said Bea with annoyed certainty.

Bounty gave Bea a quizzical look and said, "You didn't see me?" Then she smiled broadly. "Never mind. Sit beside me. Your little Sweetie needs rest after all his barking inside the pagoda."

Bea stared at Bounty with eyes wide and her

mouth open in astonishment. Certain no one sat on the bench before she entered the pagoda, she could not think of a response to Bounty's obvious fabrication.

"Let me begin. You will be happy with a story about animals you know? Yes, chickens, live chickens. You don't know about live chickens? Well, they can be difficult to handle. You grew up in the city where the only chicken you've met is wrapped in plastic or in a big greasy bucket. Too bad you haven't met real live chickens," she said with a pleasant chuckle. The lavender flower spike bobbed on her straw hat as she nodded knowingly at Bea.

Bea wondered about Bounty's proclaimed knowledge about chickens. *"Suppose I must humor her."*

Bounty began the second story in a fast flow of words, her lilting Hispanic accent strong and clear.

10

DAY TWO—THE STORY OF A FLOOD

BOUNTY

First about the flood, then the chickens, and then the wonderful part. My mamá lived through many disasters, but the flood she would never forget. A slow moving flood, but a very bad flood. She already knew hardship—she'd lost her mamá, papá and brother that terrible day in the jungle. An orphan with no choice but to go to another family member, Mamá went to live with a cousin on her papá's side. He lived about ten miles away from a pretty town. Well, pretty until the government exploded most of the buildings during the wars. Cousin Mano, who took her in, wanted her to help with the chickens. So my mamá worked on her second cousin's chicken farm so she could eat well and have a place to stay until she grew old enough to be on her own. Of course, it wasn't comfortable like you mean! People in that country did not have comfortable lives, just hard ones. The electricity for the farm went only into the farmhouse. The power did not work well all the time. They pumped water by hand from a well and collected rain in barrels for themselves and the chickens.

The season of the cold rains came early that year. My mamá said the family complained about how long it rained and all the neighbors worried about the river that ran between the farms and the town. Every year the river would spread out over its banks during the rainy time, but this year people were afraid of a bigger flood. The farmhouse sat on the highest part of the land her cousin rented from the landowner, but the chicken pens and their little shelters were in a lower area downhill. Mano decided to build a new large pen closer to the farmhouse. He labored for three days in the rain. Mano's wife insisted that my mamá also help with the building. She resented my mamá living with them even though my mamá worked very hard feeding all the chickens and cleaning out the pens. Mamá also pumped water for the house and cooked the breakfast every morning before other work began. Mano said that they must stop for one day when the rains came even harder and the mud became impossibly deep. The water from the river rose every day closer to the boundary of his land. Mano said they must pray to the Virgin for help to stop the rains long enough for him to finish the new pens and move the chickens.

That night while the family slept, the river rose quickly. When dawn came, my mamá and her cousins looked at a large lake covering the old chicken pens. Floating in the water were the bodies of all the chickens, slowly bobbing up and down in the murky black river waters. The flood had been silent and deadly. Mamá cried as Mano's wife screamed at him that they would have no money and would soon starve with all the chickens gone. My mamá hid in her room for the rest of the morning while the waters receded leaving the dead brown and red chickens covered with buzzing flies. A stray spotted dog wandered into the pens and carried off a chicken carcass into the jungle. By the afternoon Mano brought a large barrel close to the pen and worked with Mamá to pick up the dead chickens and throw them into the barrel. The smell—*muy* terrible. Her cousin's *bruja* wife sat in the farmhouse and stared out the window, her face set as stone. After a little time passed, her cousin told her to keep working and he would to talk to his wife. He wanted to calm her and persuade her to come help with the messy cleanup of the pens. Mano stayed in the house for a long time. Mamá needed rest and sat down on a large rock near a small tree swept down into the yard during the flood. Something unusual caught her eye. A rusty little box stuck in the branches of the tree. The box, partially opened, spilt out seven small objects wrapped in sodden rags. She knew in her heart the angels meant for her find the box after the disaster of the flood. She took three of the objects and placed them in her working apron. Then scooping up the box with the other four objects, she ran to the farmhouse to show her cousin what washed up in the flood. Yes, yes, the small objects were little dolls carved by native people many, many years ago. Her cousin rejoiced when he unwrapped the little dolls inside the box. His brother-in-law, a trader in the city, would pay him well for bringing the little treasures to him. The family would have enough money to last the winter and buy chickens to start up the business again. Mamá learned later it was illegal to sell and buy such old objects, yet the black market remained strong. The government could not control everything. She paid attention to what Mano said and knew the three ancient treasures she hid in her apron would see her through whatever might come into her life. A flood may sweep away what one feels is indispensable, but a flood may also bring something into your life. You can see some of the tiny dolls in the museum across the river if you want to see how valuable and ancient they are. The signs on them say "Pre-Columbian" which means very old and made by people who lived in the jungles. My mamá made the best of a very hard time. A treasure, that's what she found, and it gave her hope that she could overcome her losses and grief.

**

"Well, another story for you to have in your heart. It looks like your little dog is ready to continue his walk for the day," Bounty smiled at Bea with a radiant look on her face. Bea sat stony faced thinking about the strange story and if this really happened to Bounty's mother. *Seemed far-fetched to find a treasure after a flood that killed a bunch of chickens.* Bounty gathered up the bags of bread and tossed a last handful to the waiting birds on the lawn close by.

"Your stories are very different I must say. Now what country are you from?" Bea said in a nicer tone of voice than her usual brusque speech.

"Didn't say and doesn't matter. My family's lived here in the city for a long time. It is not where we came from but who we are that matters."

"I'm not sure what you mean. Please explain!" Bea demanded.

"Maybe another day if we meet again." Bounty picked up the bags of bread, gathered up her long white skirt and rose from the bench. "Our time is up." She strolled up the gravel path towards the pagoda.

Bea grabbed Sweetie's leash and stood to her feet. She did not like being dismissed like that. As she reached the paved path she looked back over her shoulder but she could no longer see Bounty. A bright glare dazzled her eyes for a moment, so she turned back and continued her way to the apartment. Sweetie walked obediently beside her and never once tried to stop and sniff bushes along the way. Bea's thoughts about the morning and the story were in turmoil, ranging from disbelief to indignation and back again.

11

DAY TWO—TUESDAY

CAROL

On Tuesday public school classes were over an hour earlier than other days. Teachers spent their time in service, whatever that meant. All the kids thought the teachers got to take off early, too. The shorter school day meant that Carol would have an extra hour in the park. Before she gathered her notebooks and stuffed them in her red backpack, she turned to the page in her sketch book where she had drawn a small horse that pranced in front of a bubbling spring. In the grass surrounding the spring she'd drawn little green sprouts which she hoped looked like onions. She hadn't yet sketched in a horn on the animal's head to change it into a unicorn. The story the hip girl told her had stirred her imagination. She wanted to check the same area to see if Charity, as she called herself, showed up. Carol tried not to get her hopes up too much. Random things happen and she would probably never see the girl again. She kept the encounter a secret from her mom. Her mom had been absorbed in her search for a cheaper place to live and didn't have much time in the evening to talk with Carol. A few of her mom's work friends suggested several apartments, but they were out of Carol's current school district. Carol begged not to change schools. Every time she thought about such a big change she got a sick feeling in her stomach. Her mom said she understood how Carol felt. They tried to keep it together for each other, but the stress affected them both. Her dad called twice in the last week but would not tell his whereabouts. He said that his two girls needed to start another life without him since he couldn't do it anymore. From these last calls, it sounded to Carol like their life as a family lay in ruins.

Leaving the school building, Carol walked as slowly as she could to the park. With extra time today she tried to be more observant of certain things, like trees. Her teacher told her that a good artist should study nature to get ideas. She hadn't been pleased with the trees she'd drawn in her picture of the prancing horse, which should have been a unicorn. She wanted to look at tree leaves and tree trunks to learn how to properly sketch them. No one was around to notice a young girl who walked up to a tree and stood with a pad in hand to draw the ridges and whorls in the tree's trunk. In fact, Carol felt most of the time that no one noticed her at all even when she was around other people in the park. Except, that is, for the girl on the bench yesterday. After drawing three different types of tree trunks she continued her walk toward the old bench. Once she came to the gravel path, she felt excited about seeing the friendly teenager again. Yes, someone sat on the bench. The shade from the nearby trees made it hard to see. Carol started to run and then stopped herself. *How silly. I don't really know it's her. Why would she return to the bench today?*

Charity sat patiently as Carol approached, swinging her backpack on one arm and holding a sketch pad in the other. Carol tried to act like she had happened by.

"Oh, hi." Charity flipped her braids to one side when she spoke.

"Hi." Carol's voice squeaked as she tried to act

not interested.

"What are you drawing today? Want to show me?"

"Nope."

"OK, whatever."

"Uh...Charity, that's your name, right? I liked the story you told me yesterday."

"I have been told I can tell it straight."

"Straight? Mmmmm...your story was kind of twisted."

"Twisted? Maybe you didn't catch the meaning."

Embarrassed that Charity said she hadn't understood, Carol wanted to change the subject.

"I like your shoes," she said.

Charity wore shiny silver slippers that looked great, and she was dressed again today in black sports gear. Knowing black a "fashionable" color, Carol felt awkward in her school uniform. In her white blouse and plaid skirt she knew she looked like a kid and, besides, she had on plain white tennis

"Yeah, they get me around." Charity looked surprised at Carol's comment about her shoes.

Carol plunged on with another question to cover how uncomfortable she felt.

"Do you always shuffle those cards?"

"Yeah, kid, I do. It's a habit I have. Better this one than others."

"Don't call me kid, please. I'm Carol. Do the cards help you tell stories?"

Charity ignored the remark about calling Carol "kid". "Hey, just lighten up. And yeah, the cards help me tell my stories. Does it bother you?"

"Nope, just wondering."

"Well, now you got it. I think you want to hear another one of my twisted stories, right?"

"That's great if you have time today!"

"I have time and you have even more time today. Come on, sit down. I'll try really hard to untwist a story for you."

"Will it be about your family again? You know, the one in China or wherever."

"It's always about family in one way of another. And ourselves, too. So listen up, OK?"

Charity continued to shuffle the cards as she began the story.

12

DAY TWO—THE STORY OF A FLOOD CHARITY

Shall I start with once upon a time again? Not! This is a story about a flood. My grandmother's name was Chun Tao, which translates "Spring Peach." She always told me her father named her that because spring peaches grew in the province where he grew up. Yeah, over there they are called provinces, not states. Haven't you studied world history, yet? Yeah, it is boring. Anyway, she had been taken to her second cousin's farm in the valley across the mountain from where she had lived with her parents. You know, after the terrible thing that happened. And yeah, the unicorn thing—fortunate for her, but sad. Lots of her cousins were farmers just like her parents had been. I guess they were called peasants at the time, really poor, and most of the kids didn't have to go to school, only work on the farms. The cousin's farm raised pigs that were sold at markets in the closest town. When Grandmother talked about her family home, she described a beautiful valley with mountains towering nearby. Living on the pig farm, she missed her mountain village life. A second cousin and his wife had adopted her as their own daughter since they were childless. They gave her the family name of Ying. None of her older aunts and uncles wanted to take her in after the massacre. No, I don't want to describe the massacre...it's what happened to her family. Stop interrupting the story, OK? It's hard work on a pig farm, but better if you were a daughter and not just a hired farm girl. Often the hired girls were treated badly but her cousin was a good man and glad to have a daughter. He told her he wanted someone to look after him when he got to be an old man. That is how she would fulfill her debt of adoption by him. He would tell her, and this is how she imitated him, "Ying Chun Tao, you're my daughter now. You will take care of me. Good daughter's duty to adopted father. You may call me Second Father." She said he told her about her duty quite often, but she didn't mind since she had plenty of food and a roof over her head. She willingly worked on the farm in addition to attending the local school for girls. Classes for girls met two days a week, but at least was two days of learning, not pig farming. Remember, I told you how girls were treated then. Girls like us today would be pretty unhappy about the whole situation. There are laws about schools for kids now. And you get to go to school every day and learn lots of stuff you need in this world.

In the early days of winter, rain fell for days and days. The weather there can be very cold. Feeding pigs was a hard job in the wet cold weather, but she did it every day without whining. She knew her duty. The rains were unrelenting, and the ground became very muddy. Very hard on pig business. The nearby rice fields flooded above their banks from all the rain. The farmers were out even at night trying to save the rice they could so there would be enough food for the rest of the winter. The rice fields were cut out into terraces in the sides of the hills and looked really pretty. She showed me pictures once of rice fields, like a green stairway climbing step-by-step into a foggy mountain top. The farmers, too, were worried about the dam higher up in the hills. Second Father said the dam was old but never failed in all its years.

The dam had been built in the time of his grandfather. Yeah, yeah, that's how long they lived in that place, in one valley in the mountains of the province. Weird, huh? People stayed in one place all their lives!

The morning the dam started leaking and the upper rice paddies totally overflowed from the rain was a morning Grandmother never forgot. The water caused a giant mudslide to rush down the hill into the pig pens. It started before dawn when the family awoke to terrible squealing sounds. The pig pens were filling with dark thick mud. Dozens of pigs tried to climb their way to higher ground outside the pen but the stone wall around the pen was slick with the mud. The more they tried to climb over the wall, the more the pigs slipped back and fell back into the rushing sea of mud. Mother pigs pushed with all their might and weight and little pigs were pushed back into the slippery mess and underneath the large mothers. Second Father saw the pigs' frantic thrashing to escape from the mud. He ran to the pens and to try to save the pigs. Grandmother ran to help but the terrified pigs frightened her. Two neighbors came from nearby homes and tried to help but gave up when they realized the pigs were doomed. The pigs were dead, covered with mud and all sort of other stuff that came down from the hills. Grandmother and Second Father's wife sat on the ground and cried for a long time after the men left. They wailed in grief for the pigs. Without the pigs they would not have a way to survive the winter without going into debt which Second Father said he would never do. Saying you would never do something and never doing it are two different things, correct? Oh, you think there might be a good part to come? You like happy endings to stories? Grow up, kid. Sometimes you get one and sometimes you don't. Well, this next part is pretty good. Two large mother pigs were discovered barely alive after the mudslide stopped. They were butchered as soon as they could be pulled from the muddy pens. They survived by laying on the top of the pile of other dead pigs pushed up against the stone wall. They were really hurt bad so they wouldn't have lived another day. Everyone who helped with the process received some pig meat. You know you have to butcher pigs really quickly. Ugh, hard to think about, right? That's why I am a vegetarian though Grandmother told me I'm nuts to refuse to eat meat. Grandmother had nightmares all her life about the piles of pigs, how ugly they were dying, thrashing each other, and squealing piteously until the sounds got fainter and fainter and then stopped. Over the next days the mud dried and neighbors offered to help Second Father carry off the dead pigs into the woods and bury the filthy bloated bodies.

After a week the pens were still very muddy, but with the pigs all gone Grandmother was told to pick up the debris that remained after the flood. There were dead rice plants, small pebbles, even some larger rocks washed down by the water. She found a large wooden bowl half buried at the back of the pen. When she dug it out...guess what? She found a treasure! You don't believe in finding treasure? You're very cynical for your age. I thought you wanted something good to happen, so listen up. Under a large wooden bowl lay a dirty bundle of silk rags, tightly wrapped and bound with strong cord. The bundle looked very old. The bottom half of the bundle stuck out of the mud, After digging around it with her hoe, she pulled with all her strength and freed it. She carried the bundle into the farmhouse to show Second Father, but he and his wife had gone to the upper rice paddies with the other neighbors to check the flood damage. All the farmers needed to plan for repairs before spring planting time. Grandmother told me she knew Second Father would have wanted her to wait to unwrap the bundle until he came home, but her curiosity grew strong. With a large knife from the kitchen table she cut the cord. Inside the filthy rags were five small bronze urns with tiny characters etched on the sides. Her basic education at the girls' school had not taught her to read all the characters, but she recognized the inscriptions as the old language.

Second Father and Wife arrived later and found her sitting on the floor holding the urns. "Look, look! I found a treasure in the pig pens. The old ancestors must have sent them to us," she cried. Sure, ancestors were something they believed in, and my grandmother still does.

Second Father pronounced Ying Chun Tao his lucky daughter and praised her for finding the treasure. The old urns would be sold to antique dealers for enough money to buy new pigs and seeds for the spring. Second Father praised his adopted daughter for her honesty.

Grandmother told me the story many times until one day she told me the true ending. Before Second Father returned, she hid two urns in her belongings. She said the ancestors told her to provide for herself. Second Father always believed she found only three urns. If Second Father tried to marry her off to a cousin she disliked or to an old man she did not know, she could run away to the city and sell the precious urns. She never told me if that's what she did, but then she never told me how she left the pig farm.

**

"So there you have it. Pigs, death, and treasure. That's the end of the story. Another day, another lesson. How did you like this story?"

"Wasn't your grandmother disloyal to the family who took her in by keeping two urns for herself?" The story made Carol wonder about Chun Tao's good character.

"Survival, survival. Staying alive. Planning for hard times ahead." Charity nodded as she spoke. She acted as if she had to explain a simple idea to a dense person.

Carol did not like being talked to like that, but then she had asked a lot of questions and interrupted the story.

"I am not a kid, you know. I've learned some lessons about survival!"

"I know you're trying to survive. That's why you need stories."

Charity stopped shuffling the cards. A comforting calm wrapped Carol and Charity in silence.

"Carol, you'll be late again if you don't start back now."

"Oh, sure. Guess you're right. See you later. Uh, Charity, why don't you have a Chinese name?"

"Too many questions for now. Maybe more answers another time. You'd better go now."

The teenager dressed in all black and wearing silver slippers rose quickly from the bench, adjusted her black beret and long braids, and strolled up the gravel path toward the pagoda. Carol picked up her sketch book lying on the bench beside her and stuffed it into her backpack. By the time she looked up again, Charity was gone.

13

DAY THREE—WEDNESDAY

ALICE

The last two nights Alice had not slept well due to worry and a frightening nightmare. One of her worries was deadlines for three required papers at 4 p.m. She hadn't completed all the necessary research on any of the subjects. Yesterday had been a disaster. The classes bored her, and she sat through the time without entering one word on her laptop for class notes. She knew that other students often surfed the net or watched videos during class, but until now she'd been conscientious in her attendance and performance. After class she tried to stir up her interest by dropping by her professor's office to discuss new ideas of analyzing city street patterns.

Dr. Skinner grimly informed her that appointments were required. He put her on his schedule for a time next week. Hardly likely she would keep that date the way she felt after the conversation. He treated her like a bumpkin from the Midwest who unwittingly intruded on a sacred tenet of grad school etiquette. She remembered the days in undergrad when teaching assistants and tenured professors were interested in interactions with the students. *Of all things, they smiled when a student showed up at their office.*

Alice's other big worry was school finances. Again last night a nightmare recurred about failure to complete her education. She dreamed she was dressed in a bright red graduation gown standing in front of a large wooden door shouting and crying as she pounded on the door until her fists were bloody. An oversized black lettered sign on the door said "No Admittance to Graduation for Alice." She understood why she had the dream. Last spring she had been in a panic after her mother informed her there would no more funds available for her education. Her mother told her after her father's sudden death that money for her college expenses were reserved in a special account. She assumed the designated funds covered both undergraduate and graduate school. The only daughter of a well- respected surgeon at the largest medical facility in the Midwestern city, Alice's parents provided her a comfortable life, but she never felt entitled. Entitled was a buzz word among many hardworking college students whom she met as an undergrad. They jokingly accused her of that status since her mother paid the total of her tuition and board. To make a point with her friends, Alice took a part-time job waiting tables at a chic restaurant three nights a week. The extra money came in handy as she learned what it meant to work; yet, she knew she had back-up resources during her college years that many of her friends did not.

However, back-up security came to a sudden halt when her mother met Jeff just after Alice's college graduation. Jeff changed her mother's life. She reveled in the attention of a younger man who claimed to be head-over-heels in love with the well-to-do widow of a well-known surgeon. Jeff convinced her mother that they should travel and see the world together. After tuition and board was paid for her first semester of grad school, her mother had put the education funds into a different bank account that she called My Adventures Fund. Alice suspected for some time Jeff emotionally abused her mother and would withhold his attentions unless she complied with his wishes. The situation with her mother and her new-found traveling companion gave Alice a good reason to get away to the city for grad school. She wanted to be as far away from family drama as possible.

Alice felt relieved it was Wednesday, Hump Day, as it's affectionately called by stressed grad students—it meant another morning run to enjoy. The routine kept her sane throughout the week. She left the apartment a half hour earlier than usual.

The gravel path towards the pagoda appeared sooner than she remembered. Her unfinished work still swirled in her head. Alice wanted to run until it cleared of worries about research papers and finances. Up ahead on the beautiful bench she saw the familiar silhouette of her new friend, Angel. Seeing Angel there brought a leap of relief to her heart. *Calling someone a friend takes longer than two encounters, but that's how I feel. She's someone who loves telling fantastic stories. What a delightful way to spend a little time each morning. I must enjoy the experience, not question it.*

As Alice approached, Angel nodded at her in a reserved but friendly manner. A layer of fallen leaves covered the inside of the upturned umbrella beside the bench. Alice thought it strange since the wind hadn't been blowing and the trees around the bench were bare. Angel reached down and brushed all of the leaves out of the umbrella and primly straightened herself. The removal of leaves in the umbrella every day was a serious ritual with Angel.

"Hello again. You look tired this morning, my dear. Did you not sleep well?"

"Hello to you, Angel. Did you arrive at the park earlier today? I'm on an earlier schedule this morning, too. I have to finish up some projects before classes."

Angel ignored Alice's question about her arrival time. "Well, we should start the story for today then. This one is a short one, but you must listen carefully. It's about a journey with my father."

Taking her seat on the bench Alice leaned back and tried to relax. She would rather hear a long story that would put off her work on the projects. She didn't care much if she finished the pointless assignments or not. Most of all, she couldn't bear to think about what she would do with her life if she dropped out of school. Yes, she was ready to hear Angel's new tale and forget her worries.

Angel began.

14

DAY THREE—THE STORY OF A JOURNEY ANGEL

I had never been away from the village of my birth until one day Father announced I would take a journey with him to visit family. He hadn't been in contact with them for many years. Once when I asked why I did not have grandparents like other families, Mother replied that Father never talked about his family. The family disowned him. Mother would not explain what happened between Father and his family. I understood the subject could not be discussed. Later when I met my friend Elenna to go berry picking in the woods, she explained that if a family member is disowned that means the person did something shameful to deserve such punishment. Her uncle had been disowned when he ran away with a gypsy woman who came to the village with other Roma on a spring trading trip. He left for three years and she bore him two children during that time. When he tried to return to the family with his two young sons in tow, the family refused him entrance into his previous home. They shouted at him to leave. His brothers and sisters threw stones until he and the two children left. They would never speak of him and said he was dead to the family. Yes, that's a very harsh way for families to act. I don't know if that happened to my father. He never told anyone his story.

The day I left with Father for the journey, Mother cried and cried after us. She begged us not to go, but the decision stood. He told her his family must learn about their two grandchildren. My three year old brother Dovid was too young to make the journey so only I would travel with him. He informed me that when the family saw me their hearts would melt knowing that he had done a good thing to bring a beautiful child into the world. He was convinced the family would forgive him. It pleased me when he called me beautiful though I knew in my heart he hadn't told me the truth. I was a plain child.

We walked through the forest the first day until we came to a road rutted with deep tracks of wagons. Father walked at such a steady pace that I lagged behind and began to cry. He agreed to stop for a time. Our one stop had been at the spring for a drink of cool water. Father filled a jug with cool spring water. We had not stayed long enough to eat the food that Mother wrapped in cloths and put in his heavy knapsack. When we came to a fork in the road, we sat by the side and Father brought out two cheeses and a small loaf of bread. We ate in silence chewing on the dark bread and tasty cheese. He offered me a few sips from the jug of spring water. With the daylight almost gone, I began to wonder where we would sleep but Father did not seem concerned. "We will wait. Someone will come," he said. I had never spent a night sleeping outdoors. I was fearful of the darkness surrounding us. I worried there were no walls to keep away animals that prowled the night.

My uncle told about large grey wolves that came from the forest and killed young calves on the farm. His stories terrified me. The rest of the family would laugh at his stories, but Dovid and I believed what he said. Now, please, you have been so polite today. Why do you interrupt now? It does not matter the name of the old country. I am very sorry that you know so little about wolves. Yes, they live in the forests and would eat unguarded livestock of the villagers when there was no other prey available.

There were always rumors of wolf attacks on humans. Of course, that is why Uncle told such stories so the children would know about wolves and not be caught in the forests alone. Didn't elders in your family warn the children of dangers they might encounter? Does that answer your questions? I will never finish the story at this rate. You must listen and learn.

As the sun went down, we heard the wheels of a wagon rumbling down the road and could see two horses plodding in our direction. Father stood up by the side of the road and shouted for the person in the wagon to stop. The old man in the wagon peered down at us in the fading light and saw that we were villagers like him. An invitation to sit in the back of a passing wagon and a ride farther down the road was what Father had counted on. Yes, yes, Father wanted to get to the town, but he knew it too far for a day's walk. Have you ever walked so far in a day? Running in the park is not the same as walking all day long, my dear. Now, let me tell you more. The back of the wagon was piled high with turnips he planned to sell at market. The market opened early so the farmers came to the town in the evening and slept in their wagons. My father and I slept on the ground near the wagon that night. It was a most uncomfortable night, but we were safe. Feeling obligated for the man's kindness, we stayed for market day and helped the man unload turnips and stack them in large piles.

At the end of the day, the good farmer gave Father a few coins for our work. He left with his wagon to return to his home, leaving us to face another long walk. The city where Father's family lived was still miles away. Father sent me to ask other people with wagons at the market if we could, for a small price, ride with them if they were going in the direction we were headed. I found a young woman named Elke who accepted our offer. She planned to leave for the next town in the morning to try to sell what she had left over from the market. Her wagon was loaded with kitchen pots and pans and a few used farming tools. She was alone since her older brother, who usually drove the wagon, had been injured in a fall and wasn't able to drive until he healed. The three of us slept under her wagon that night. That night I slept soundly.

We set off at dawn the next morning with Elke in her rickety wagon. I sat most of the day in the back of the wagon with the rattling pans while Father sat up front with her and took turns handling the reins of the mule. Large brown mules are very slow, but they are steady. Once we arrived at the city we thanked her for her kindness and Father paid her one shiny coin. I will never forget how grateful she was to receive that one coin. The first city I had ever seen bustled with activity and busy people. Father attended school there in his youth. His parents sent him to a great teacher to learn Torah. Father would only say that the experience wasn't what he hoped it would be, but he would not say what it was. The city overlooked a large river with a suitable port for smaller trading barges that traveled up and down the river weekly to bring supplies and goods in exchange for farm produce, cheeses, and meats produced by the local people. Yes, I was very naïve and had never seen boats and rivers until then. Father said if we rode on a barge downriver we would come to a much larger city where his parents lived.

Father persuaded one of the boatmen to let us ride downriver, but he made a bad choice of choosing a barge full of pigs. All day long we sat on the roof of the barge with the fetid smell of pigs while we floated nearer and nearer to our anticipated family reunion. Arriving in the city late in the afternoon, I couldn't stop myself from scrambling off the barge as fast as I could, desperate to get away from the smelly pigs. Father found an inn where we ate bowls of hot soup, warm bread and one delicious cheese. We washed as best we could at the fountain close to the inn and brushed dust from our clothes. We wanted to be presentable to his family. Father acted very nervous about the impending meeting. The streets were filled with carts and horses jostling people and shops displaying many useful items. Wonderful aromas came from small shops that offered food for sale. You can imagine my amazement at all the uproar. It was so unlike the peaceful village I knew. We walked for an hour until we came to a quieter section of homes. Dusk enveloped the unfamiliar streets. We saw lamps glowing in the windows of the houses. Father looked up and down one street several times and then spoke to me in a quiet whisper. "My family lives in that house, the big one on the corner. That's where I lived when I was your age." Without another word, we walked to the heavy wooden door with its large brass knocker. Father held me up and told me to bang the brass knocker as loud as I could.

**

"Oh my, the story has gotten quite long for today. You keep looking at your watch. Why don't I stop and you can imagine the ending for yourself. No, no, I understand how pressed for time you must be. No, I won't finish the story. You can make what you want of it."

Angel reached down abruptly and shut the umbrella. A few leaves that had drifted close to the umbrella were caught in the outside folds. She looked at Alice for a few moments as if to imply that Alice should leave. Alice checking her watch had somehow offended Angel. She sat with a faint smile on her face waiting for Alice to make the next move.

"Well, I think I can guess how the story ended. The family had long since moved away and you never met them. The journey was in vain." Alice's voice had a tinge of disappointment.

"That's the best ending you can come up with? Don't you know that journeys represent something in our lives? Was the tale about rejection or something else?"

"I hoped it would be about reconciliation of your family. That would be a happy ending."

"Not all of life has a happy ending, young woman. You need to learn the definition of happiness. And you need to learn to seize happiness while you can."

Alice sighed and stood up to leave. Angel picked up her umbrella and rose unsteadily to her feet. She swayed slightly and then seemed to compose herself as she turned to walk away. A veil of silence came between them. Alice bent over to tie the loosened laces on her running shoes. When she straightened up and looked down the path Angel was not in sight.

15

DAY THREE—WEDNESDAY

BEA

Bea arose early on Wednesday morning. Trash cans had to be taken to the curb for weekly pick-up. The building super did not allow residents to put the cans out the night before—too many stray dogs and drunks passing by. If a resident put a trash can on the curb in the evening, the super would come to their apartment as late as midnight and insist the resident take the container back inside. Bea had slept fitfully all night, waking from vivid dreams about floating chickens and big breasted dolls that danced through green jungles. After hearing the story from the happy woman in the park who called herself Bounty, Bea looked in old National Geographic magazines she had in her closet and found photographs of ancient pre-Columbian figures roughly carved in stone. The little dolls were in museums all over the world and were priceless artifacts. She saw that the female dolls had huge breasts. The magazine said they were fertility symbols to pre-historic Indians of Central and South America. The facts made sense to Bea. Bounty was Hispanic and her parents must have lived in one of those countries. Bea surprised herself that she took the time to see if the information matched what Bounty had told her about the valuable figures. Maybe she would go up to the museum on 88th Avenue one day to look at the displays.

Bea worked with many Hispanics in the City Tax Office. She did not know why they called themselves different names. Hispanic, Latin, Mexican, Spanish, it all seemed the same to her. The workers' fluency in many dialects was highly prized since so many different languages were spoken in the city. Bea sometimes wondered what language her ancestors spoke, the ones who came on the ships across the Atlantic hundreds of years ago. Black people like her could sometimes trace back their family to some particular Southern slave owner, but most never spoke about African homelands. Bea hadn't thought about those things in many, many years, not since her younger days in high school when she attended a racially integrated school in the close suburbs. Her parents saved enough money to purchase a modest home in a decent neighborhood. They were the third black family to move in. Now, years later, only black families lived there since the whites had fled over the years to far-flung suburbs where they said they felt safe. Bea always felt safe in her neighborhood because everyone was the same class. Friends and neighbors were middle class hardworking people who drove buses, cleaned houses, swept offices at night, cut hair in the barber shops, served meals, watched children, and led what she thought a fairly decent life. Only as a teenager had she discovered the problems of young black kids once they left the safe street of the neighborhood.

Bea ate her usual breakfast of toast, half an apple, and four cups of strong black coffee. The doctor told her during her annual exam that so much coffee probably made her irritable. She laughed at him and said, “That’s just my way, Doc.” She was rather proud of her ill-temper. The doctor shrugged and completed his exam in silence. Most people, even professionals, didn’t engage Bea for long periods. She was a hard person to abide.

Around eleven o’clock Bea became restless and wandered the apartment. She straightened magazines, opened blinds and shut them, wiped the kitchen counter four times, rinsed out the coffee pot. She realized that she was eager to leave for the morning walk in the park. *Bounty might be there. Maybe they could sit on the bench together without any strange stories, just feeding the pigeons and petting Sweetie.* That's the kind of person Bea preferred to be around, a quiet person, one not so eager to share personal family tragedies. After all, Bounty's tales had been about all her mother, Blanca. If Bounty did not show up, she would have the bench all to herself and that would be just fine with Bea, too. She would let Sweetie off leash to chase those dreadful pigeons away from the path.

Sweetie strained at the leash through the first part of their walk. Dogs know when regular schedules change or when their owners upset a routine. The park seemed more deserted than usual today. Bea remembered something about a big sale at the discount clothing store a few blocks away. Maybe she should go there later in the afternoon and see if the housedresses she favored were on sale. She needed to buy a larger size. She completely ignored the doctor's comment about her fifteen pound weight gain. *Things just shifted around on my body,*

When Bea got closer to the gravel path that turned off, suddenly the park looked different. She was sure the way to the pagoda was by the two big oak trees whose tops arced across the path, but she couldn't see the trees or the path. Sweetie began running back and forth following the trail of some other creature. Bea didn't see any squirrels.

"What is it, Sweetie? Where's our little path? Come on, puppy, we'll turn around." After retracing her steps, she saw the gravel path and the two trees. "Humph, I missed the turn, Sweetie. How'd I do that?" she said, as she turned onto the fine gravel that wound toward the old broken down pagoda.

Her watch showed 11:30 a.m. and there sat Bounty on the bench tossing crumbs to the pigeons. Bea wasn't sure if she was aggravated or relieved. *What's with the white dress anyway? Doesn't she know white isn't a color for cool weather?* Bea read that advice long ago in some fashion magazine and it stuck with her. *Or maybe that was a Southern custom her auntie told her about. Something about being a respectable lady. Odd thing was that Bounty said her mother's name was Blanca—that means white in Spanish.* She doubted Bounty's mamá ever knew about etiquette for wearing white if her mother lived in the jungle. These thoughts reeled in Bea's head as she and Sweetie approached closer to the bench. Bounty noticed her, gave a cheery wave, and grinned at her with a look of pure happiness.

"Hola...uh, hello, I mean. Sorry you did not sleep well last night. Bad dreams, no?"

Bea wasn't sure she heard correctly. *How did Bounty know she'd not slept well and had bad dreams? Maybe I look tired from dreaming about those big boob dolls.*

"Please, please rest for a minute before you continue on your walk. I think little dog needs a drink of water. Look how he's panting."

"Dogs always pant." She didn't want to talk about Sweetie's panting so she said it firmly to let Bounty know she wouldn't discuss it anymore. "And why are you here so early?"

"Am I before time? Being early means there is more time, yes?"

"I always keep a routine and I assumed you did, too. We've seen each other at the same time for two days. Today we're both here early." Bea made matter-of-fact statements.

"Being early means you want to hear another good story today? It's about a journey my mamá once took with her papá."

"Didn't you say your mother was named Blanca? Is that the color white?"

"Of course. Are you learning Spanish now that

you retired from your job?"

I never told her I retired. She must have guessed since I walk Sweetie in the middle of the day. Bea's face did not betray her surprise about Bounty's comment.

"Yes I'm retired and I think you are, too."

"No, no, I keep working all my days. It's what I'm meant to do."

"What is it you do?"

"Why do you ask?" said Bounty with a puzzled look on her face. "You know what I do. I tell you stories. Now let me tell you the story about the long journey my mamá took with her papá to find the lost family."

"Her family was lost?"

Bounty gave a big laugh. "You don't understand lost. I mean lost to her papá. That's what happened."

Before Bea could utter another word, Bounty began the story.

16

DAY THREE—THE STORY OF A JOURNEY BOUNTY

Once when my mamá, Blanca, was still a young girl, she went on a long journey. Most people did not travel long distances from their villages, especially the children until they were much older or until the boys ran away to join the soldiers. I can never remember what they were fighting about or where they went to fight, but mamá said the boys always left. OK, what is your question about the boys? Sure, some came home and some were killed. Back to my story that I heard from my mamá. The journey would take several days. There were many arguments between her parents about taking Blanca on such a journey. Her mamá argued she was too young and would be frightened being away from her home. Her papá insisted that he must take her along. She was the reason for the journey. He told her his family had disowned him many years ago. He married her mamá against their wishes and went to live with his cousins. The cousins were farmers and welcomed him and his bride as they were hard workers. You never know anyone disowned? Very bad thing to happen in the family. *Si*, being separated from your family by other people who owned you is a very bad thing, too. Those bad things have happened to many families in many countries. The history of your family must be full of family stories, yes?

Well, Mamá told me that her papá said it was time for his family to know he had done good things, worked hard and had a lovely daughter, a grandchild to be proud of in their old age. Everyone wants to know about a granddaughter, even family who are angry and stopped talking to each other. I heard this story many times, but the last time she told it she added that her mamá feared the family would insist on keeping their granddaughter in the city and would take her away from Benito. That was her papá's name. Benito means blessed one. The family cursed him when they disowned him, but he didn't change his name. And yes, every time Mamá told me this story, it was in the language of her country, Spanish.

The preparations were made for the journey after the arguments stopped. My grandmother Constanza packed food for the journey in a large bag. There were fruits, tortillas, and beans to eat on the first day. What did her name mean? You like knowing names, Bea. Translated name means "steadfast." She would have been a steadfast person to agree to marry a disowned man. Back to my story, please. They left early in the morning to walk through the jungle to a main road. The road led to the city where his family lived. Mamá had never been as far as the main road before, but others in the village traveled the road after the harvests. There were many stories told to the children to make them afraid of going through the jungle. Stories of large jaguars that would follow a person for miles before jumping on top of them and tearing out the throat to kill them. No one ever found anyone with their throat torn out from a jaguar attack, but stories were told to keep the children from wondering off from the safe village. During the long day in jungle with her papá, the walk was hard but not frightening. She said she felt safe because Benito was a large strong man and carried his machete with him. No prowling jaguar would dare attack them.

Yes, I've seen a jaguar in zoo once. You should go to a zoo. It's good thing and teaches you about animals. Are laughing at me? I don't think unicorns were ever in the zoo. I'll go on with story about mamá's journey. *Gracias*.

Papá Benito planned for his cousin to meet him at a certain spot by the banana trees on the main road. The cousin came as he had promised with his wagon. My mamá was so happy that they could sit in the wagon. She had never walked so far as she did that day. The cousin's wagon carried fruits to sell at the market. Even today I can almost smell the fruits she described. Yes, some bananas, that's the smell. Maybe other fruits that grew on the trees, too. She fell asleep riding in the wagon and did not remember coming to the town or her papá taking her to the fruit market.

When she woke up in the morning, the people were already arriving at the market. Her papá and his cousin stacked the lovely fruits high on a large table. At the end of the day the cousin gave them five shiny copper coins for helping him. He said Blanca's beauty helped sales. Many people stopped by his table to see the beautiful child who held up the nice fruits and smiled at everyone. The memories of selling fruit were very happy ones for my mamá.

The second night away from her home Mamá spent at a very small house that belonged to their cousin's friend. She and her papá slept on the floor on blankets and shared a bowl of corn stew. The next morning before they left to continue the journey her papá thanked the friend and paid him a small coin. On the third day they walked across the town looking at many big houses close together and shops that sold many beautiful and strange things she did not recognize. There were more people than she had ever seen. Her papá held her hand all day and she felt safe. For the first time she heard people speaking a language she didn't understand. Yes, it was tongue of the *Norte Americanos. Si,* English, of course. My mamá finally learned English when she grew old in this country.

At last, they reached the edge of the town that ended by a very large lake. On the lake were many barges and boats that carried goods and people. Her papá told her there was another town across the lake and that is where they were going for the reunion with his family. He reminded her that she was an important part of the reunion and would make the family very happy to see her, such a beautiful granddaughter. "If a disowned son brought back a lovely granddaughter, the family would forgive him and all would be right again," he told her. The trip across the lake was not something Mamá remembered with happiness. The ride in the rocking boat made her very sick. She spent time lying down in the bottom of the boat. It was a boat built for people to ride in back and forth across the large lake. Four other people sat on the benches with Papá and silently watched the man row the boat. As she lay in the bottom of the boat she closed her eyes and prayed. When they reached the other side, she sat down on the grass and sipped water from a leather water bag. She couldn't eat the food her papá tried to give her. He let her rest on the grass by the lake until the rocking inside her stomach stopped and she could stand by herself. Mamá would never go on a boat again for the rest of her life.

The trip across the lake took longer time than Benito planned. The sun was setting on the horizon as they reached the edge of the town where the reunion would happen. Fortunately, the part of the town where his family lived lay close to the lake. Papá told her it was not too far to walk and hopefully they would arrive before dark. They walked on cobblestone streets lined with houses that were taller than she had ever seen. Windows and doors were street level, but she also looked in amazement at windows high above her head. Later she understood that these were houses with two floors, but at the time she didn't know about two story buildings. As

Mamá and her papá came to a large house on a corner, he asked her to start singing a little song he had taught her on the journey through the jungle. She had not been able to practice when she felt sick crossing the lake. The little song came from his mother who sang it to him as a boy. When they arrived at the large wooden door of the house, her papá put her on the front step. He stepped back into the shadows after he rang the large brass bell that hung by the door. "Keep singing, my daughter. Keep singing," he urged. Yes, Blanca, my mamá, kept singing the song over and over. All at once, the heavy wooden door creaked open and a very old woman peered out. With a great frown the woman looked at my mamá on the steps. The woman's eyes were clouded and she strained to see who stood at the door singing so beautifully. "Benito? Is it you Benito?" she asked. "Have you repented of your ways and returned?" At that moment, my grandfather, Benito stepped from the shadows and said, "I have brought your granddaughter, beautiful Blanca. The song you taught me as a child will mend our hearts. Please forgive me and I will forgive you." My mamá stopped singing and the old woman opened the heavy door.

**

"What do you think, Bea? I see your Sweetie dog getting restless and wants to run again. No, no, that is not the end of story, but you can imagine it, can't you? You must think of ending of your story. Who do you forgive? OK, *mi amiga*. I must be on my way. The story went *muy* long."

Bounty was on her feet and wrapped up the half empty bag of bread she had brought for the pigeons. She adjusted the white straw hat on her head and looked down at Bea still sitting on the bench. Without a word of goodbye, she walked up the path toward the pagoda, turned a bend around a clump of tall bushes and disappeared from sight. Bea sat on the bench for a long while until Sweetie stood on his little legs and shook so much that Bea felt a wave of sympathy for her little pet that she had never felt before. "Come, Sweetie," she sighed. "Not much else to do here. Let's go home." Sweetie perked his ears when he heard the word "home". Bea bent over and saw Sweetie's inquisitive look. She whispered to him, "The story made me very sad. My family never found each other. They didn't know where to look."

17

DAY THREE—WEDNESDAY

CAROL

Before Carol left the apartment that morning, she mentioned to her mom that she walked through the park before she got home. She did not explain that she stayed in the park for as long as possible until just before her mom returned from work. For some reason, her mom made no comment about safety. Carol was satisfied she'd been honest but she had the feeling her mom was so distracted she hadn't heard what she said. *Oh well, I told her so she can't be mad. And I'm never late and always get home in time to have her tea ready the minute she comes in the door.* In the past her dad made tea for her mom after work. Now she felt responsible for the small task that made her mom so happy. They called it

Our Ritual. They enjoyed sipping hot tea and talking about the day. She really missed her dad and those times before all the fighting began.

Wednesdays and Fridays were Carol's favorite school days. Miss Brandt, the friendly young art teacher, taught sixth period. Carol's favorite subject was art and she wished art class was offered every day but middle school art budgets had been cut. Former teachers had encouraged her obvious talent. Her mom once talked about paid lessons from a private teacher after school. The money, or rather lack of money since her dad had left, ended any talk about art lessons.

All day she anticipated showing Miss Brandt the drawings she had done of objects in the park. The pagoda had been difficult for Carol. Somehow, it looked slightly different on Tuesday than on Monday when she first entered the little building and discovered the beautiful blue sky ceiling. The instructional films the teacher had shown them explained about the difference light makes when sketching outdoors. Today after school when she went to the park she wanted to pay special attention to what kind of light reflected off the pagoda.

At the beginning of art class students shared the work they did for last week's assignments. Each student presented three sketches done with either pencil or charcoal. In Carol's sketch pad were twice as many drawings as anyone else in class. When the dismissal bell rang, Miss Brandt asked Carol to stay for a few minutes to help tidy up art supplies and talk. Usually Carol did the task without her teacher asking so she was surprised at the request.

"Carol, you're showing great aptitude in this class. I talked with Mr. Perry, your teacher last year. He wanted to know how you were doing as a seventh grader."

"Mr. Perry was a really nice teacher. You're nice, too. Please tell him art is still my favorite subject."

"I have a proposal for you, Carol. Mr. Perry and I have a private studio and give art classes on Saturdays. Would you like to study with us? It's only four blocks away, close to the deli on 88th Avenue."

"I don't think I have time." Carol hung her head and looked down at her feet.

"Carol, it'd be really good for you. You have talent. Think about it and ask your mother. Please look at me, Carol."

"How much would it cost?"

"We charge what your family can afford," said Miss Brandt with an encouraging note in her voice.

"We can't afford it at all." Carol's reply was barely

audible.

“Oh, Carol. We’d figure out a way for you to earn your class fee. Maybe you could help out before and after class to get the room organized.”

“I’ll think about it. I like to do my art outdoors.”

“You would have assignments just as you do for school art class. The sketches you showed me were lovely park scenes. They looked like a park from the early twentieth century.”

“No, they were the park. You know, the one about a block away.”

“Well, you have a good imagination about what the park looked like in the early days.”

“It looks like that now. I need to go now, OK?” Carol was impatient to leave.

“Think about the art classes and ask your mother.”

“Sure. Thanks for asking me to take classes with you and Mr. Perry.” Carol forced a smile.

“Carol, you do have talent. Someday I wish you would show me that part of the park where you found that lovely old-fashioned bench.”

“It’s there. You could find it. See you Friday.”

“Bye, Carol. See you then.”

Carol could feel Miss Brandt watching her as she shouldered her faded red backpack and stepped into the hallway. She looked back and saw her teacher slowly shaking her head as she gathered her briefcase and shut off the classroom lights.

Carol ran down the front steps of P.S. 236. She had her hopes up that Charity, the super cool teenager, would be back again today. *Probably only a coincidence Charity was there for two days anyway. I bet she has other friends to meet somewhere else.* Carol was good at rationalizing why things didn't work out like she hoped they would.

When Carol walked up the path, she saw Charity on the bench in the afternoon sun. She had her feet propped up on the bench and the silver slippers sparkled as sun rays hit her feet. The worn deck of cards flew in lazy arcs from her left hand to the right and back again.

"Hi Charity! You're here again!"

"Yeah, like always. You seem happy today. Was school fun?"

"I had art class and my teacher liked my sketches of the park. But I didn't do a very good job on the pagoda."

"What was wrong with it?"

"Dunno, just didn't look good. Maybe I could sketch you? I need to practice faces."

"Would you make me look young?"

"You are young."

"Yeah, you're right. Must of forgot." Charity nodded to herself and chuckled. "I haven't had my portrait done in years."

"Someone did a portrait of you? Neat! Was it oils?"

"Yes. A long time ago. I was different then."

"Yeah, when you were a baby?"

"Sure. That's it. I was a baby."

Carol kept fidgeting from foot to foot. She wanted to pull out her pad and sketch Charity, but she hadn't understood Charity's response to her request.

"What's wrong, Carol?"

"Nothing. Can I sit on the bench?"

"Sorry. I was rude not to ask, huh?" Charity cocked her head and gave Carol a crooked smile.

Carol dropped her backpack on the ground and was about to sit down when she looked over at the pagoda. *It looked different today. It was shining, or it was glowing, or maybe it was reflecting light.* Carol felt she couldn't come up with the proper thought about how the pagoda looked.

"Why does the pagoda look different?" she asked abruptly.

"What do you mean?"

"Oh, you know, different. Must be the light on it.

Miss Brandt said light plays tricks on artists and they are always trying to capture it. I see what she meant."

"Wow! You are really into art for a kid."

"I'm not a kid, remember."

"Forgot again. Please forgive me, Carol. It just comes out." For a second time Charity gave Carol a crooked silly smile.

"Do you have time for another story? Or are you going to capture the pagoda in the light today?"

"Very funny, ha ha ha. Now you're making fun of me." Carol jokingly made a sad face.

"No, just teasing you a little. I know how serious you are about your art. Come on, sit down. I think you'll get into this story today."

Carol's eyes lit up with unsuppressed excitement. Charity began the third story.

18

DAY THREE—THE STORY OF A JOURNEY CHARITY

My grandmother Spring Peach took a long journey when she was young. I like to call her Spring Peach, remember that's what her Chinese name meant. What? You really have a thing for calling people by the name you like. You like her Chinese name and I know you don't like being called kid. I'll try to always call you Carol."

My grandmother Chun Tao took a long journey when she was young. Her father Cheng Shi, that would be my great- grandfather, announced that he intended to take his daughter to visit family far away in the city. Actually, his name meant "city born." Yep, they gave the children a name to tell something about them. His announcement took the family by surprise. Daughters didn't get special treatment. Even at a very young age, a daughter was trained to work hard and obey her elders. Not exactly like that today, right? My grandmother did not know until she was older that Cheng Shi had left his family in the city as a young man and went to the village where he met my great-grandmother. In those days, people married the person their parents approved. He broke that tradition and married a girl from the village. One old aunt said he ran away from his home because he loved someone in the city but could not marry her. Another old uncle had said he had been taken by the government and made to work in the communal fields of the province. The fact that he married without his parents' approval was a scandal for his whole family.

When the departure day arrived and her mother packed food for the trip, my grandmother clung to her mother and cried. "No, no, no. Please don't take me away, Father." The other aunts and cousins cried, too, asking why Cheng Shi would take his daughter on a trip unless it was to sell her as a bride to some rich old man. That happened in those days. An old man would buy a very young girl for a bride and keep her until she was old enough to marry. The old men wanted someone to take care of them in their old age. Who would do that? Horrible old men. Yuck! Glad that doesn't happen today.

A horse-drawn wagon waited for the travelers in the middle of the village. Cheng Shi had hired his cousin to take them to the city. The journey would take long three days. Of course, grandmother and her father weren't the only cargo. Sacks of rice were piled high in the bed of the wagon leaving very little room for the two passengers. The two horses that pulled the wagon looked like they could not walk one whole day, much less two days down from the hills into the valley to the city where his family lived. My grandmother remembered that she slept most of the time on top of a very lumpy rice sack while the two men took turns driving the horses.

The first night they stopped by a small river surrounded by dark night sounds. Stories told about roving bandits made the three villagers wary of falling asleep but the horses needed rest and water. Her father had brought a large knife to protect them and she was sure he would use it if bandits came. That was the most terrifying night my grandmother had spent...until later when other things happened.

The second night on the road was spent at a small inn that took in travelers. It was close to large rice fields where two main roads merged. Her father paid for two bowls of thin noodle soup which they ate with two small hard rice flour rolls, the last of the food from home. Great-grandfather traded a small bag of rice for the night's lodging. As they prepared to leave, the innkeeper warned them of dangers in the city. Travelers returning from the city repeated rumors that a sickness had broken out among the city residents during the summer months. Many families lost young children and elders. Her father did not seem concerned about what he had been told about the sickness. "The hot season is over," he told the man. "The people in the city will buy my cousin's rice. I am taking my little daughter to meet her relatives." The man persisted in his warning. "There have been many changes in the city recently. Do not stay long there. There are things you do not understand." Oh yeah, people thought villagers were not educated, but my great-grandfather had been to school before he ran away from his family.

It was the third day that my grandmother had been away from her mother and her home. Grandmother traveled in the back of the wagon, content to listen to her father and his cousin talk between themselves and pay her no attention. When they came to the city and found the market where the rice was sold, many of the stalls were empty. A handful of people sat glumly beside small piles of potatoes, turnips, and torn bags of rice. The smell of rotten vegetables made Grandmother hold her nose. Packs of skinny dogs nosed around the piles and no one tried to scare them away. She had never seen such disturbing sights, but then she had never been out of her village. Cheng Shi was worried and demanded that the cousin drive them in the wagon to the far edge of the city to his family home. The two men argued for a long time. Cousin wanted to go to the central district to find a government official. The government controlled what the farmers could do, you know. Rice couldn't be sold without government permission. Rules about selling stuff today? Oh sure, there are rules today. Maybe you'll have a class about that when you're in high school. It's boring, believe me.

After the argument, Cousin drove away in his wagon filled with rice bags. Grandmother and her father were stranded and had no choice but to begin walking through the city. The dusty streets had refuse tossed around, and most of the buildings were shuttered. They saw shadows of people who peeked from behind partially shuttered windows and a few old men peered at them from rooftops, but the city remained strangely silent.

Grandmother told me she would never forget the happiness that glowed on her father's face when they came to a wide avenue and turned up a narrow street to stand before a very large wooden house. The house, like many others they had passed, appeared neglected or abandoned. Her father muttered to himself something she could not hear as they approached the carved wooden doors. A large gong hung by the door. Her father picked up the mallet and struck the gong with all his might. The mighty sound made my grandmother shiver in fright. She told me she thought it was the sound of great moaning from the heavens.

"If they are here, they will answer." After waiting quietly for several minutes, he began shouting, "My family! My family! Where are you?" He rang the gong several more times, but no one came to open the wooden doors of his family home.

**

The cards in Charity's hand fell into a neat pile in her lap. "Did you like the story?"

"Scary," gulped Carol. "And what about the ending?

"Scary? Of course, there was an ending. You heard it."

Carol blinked in disbelief at what Charity said. She took a deep breath and let it out with a sigh of disappointment.

“Well, if you don’t like my ending you can tell me one that you like better.”

“Make up the ending myself? You’re the storyteller here. How do I know what happened?”

Charity shrugged and turned her palms upward in an “I give up” gesture. Carol looked at Charity in dismay.

“I can’t make up the ending of your story. That’s not how it works when you hear a story. You have to tell me what it means.”

“Sorry, if you don’t get what it means and it doesn’t seem like an ending to you. Just think about it. Say, looks like time for you to head back home. You stayed later than usual. You might not make it back in time to make tea for your mom. See you around.”

Charity got up from the bench, adjusted her long braids and walked to the grassy edge of the path toward the pagoda. She stopped and turned back around to face Carol, silent but with a faint smile on her face. Carol slumped on the bench. She didn’t understand the story at all. She shut her eyes tightly and took two deep breaths. *How did Charity know she had tea with her mother when she got home every day?*

"Please tell me the real ending," pleaded Carol in a shaky voice as hot tears gathered in the corners of her closed eyes. "I wanted the family to be together again."

She opened her eyes. "Charity?"

No one stood on the grassy edge of the path. Carol grabbed her backpack. Two books and the sketch pad fell out onto the ground. As she crammed the items back in, she kept looking around.

"Charity? Charity?"

Carol ran down the gravel as her heartbeat kept time with her footsteps. When she stopped at the turn into the main park, she looked back. She could see a dark silhouette that looked like a slender girl far up the gravel path. She caught a glimpse of the metal roof of the pagoda glinting in the late afternoon sun.

19

DAY FOUR—THURSDAY

ALICE

Thursday was the day that Alice usually slept in since her classes started late afternoon. Yet, she set her alarm for an hour earlier than usual. She wanted an early start as she had some serious thinking to do. She wondered how to stay motivated in order to finish the semester. Deadlines loomed for enrollment for next semester. She knew she must decide whether to continue with her current graduate school studies. Job prospects for someone with only an undergraduate degree were rather hopeless in the current work environment. After applying for advertised internships with large corporations, she discovered many companies today did not pay interns. Recruiters touted the advantages of a resume showing time spent as an intern at a prestigious company. *How did they expect a young person to live? Not everyone's family supported them.* When her mother stopped paying her tuition she took out loans totaling $50,000.00 with payments deferred for two years while in grad school. If she dropped out of the master's program, the loan payments would start within three months. It was all in the fine print she neglected to pay much attention to when she signed the papers. *If only things were different between me and Mom. How could she do this to me? It's not what Dad intended. What a mess.*

Alice fretted about dwindling funds and deferred payments while she watched the clock. She tried to tell herself that she wanted more exercise, not that the main reason she had arisen early was she hoped to see Angel. Today she would question Angel. *Why did Angel appear in the park at such an early hour? Where did she live? Why did she like telling fantastic stories to passing strangers? Yeah, I like being with her. Maybe I am just lonely and have projected a grandmother relationship with her.* Alice never knew her grandmother and she admitted to herself she wanted to think of Angel that way even though she had only known her for three days.

When Alice left the building that morning, she tried to put her worries aside and focus on her jog. A big bonus to her morning would be another story from Angel, her grandmother storyteller. As Alice jogged onto the gravel path she sensed something amiss. She remembered the clump of trees by the path, but she did not remember so much empty space ahead. The low stone walls that previously seemed so charming now were fallen over in disrepair. The sunlight's glare off the river made it impossible to locate the pagoda. She hadn't gone back into the lovely little structure since Monday. Today she planned to take another look. She jogged for what she thought the usual amount of time until she should reach Angel's bench. She ran on and on and still couldn't locate the bench or the pagoda. She slowed her pace as she realized that the gravel path made a loop to the right away from the river and circled a large stonework fountain.

The fountain displayed three rotund cherubs holding hands. Each cherub wore a different expression on its face—one, a smile—another, an astonished look. The third cherub's face had disintegrated with age. The entire wall around the fountain lay crumbled, the empty basin full of dead leaves and what looked like old cigar butts. She recoiled as she saw the cigar butts moving slightly. The wiggling objects were dark beetles that scrambled slowly among the dead leaves. Alice had stumbled on a different part of the park that suffered from years of neglect. *Why can't I see the pagoda? How could I have missed the iron bench? Where did I take a wrong turn?*

Alice walked slowly to get her bearings. The river water shone from the morning sun and little shimmers of waves caught the light as a small tugboat passed by. Alice sat on the grassy edge of the path and tried to calm herself. The worries of school, her financial plight, her dissatisfaction with her studies, and the alienation from her mother were piling up. Built-up stress caused her to lose her way on a simple jog in the park. As she closed her eyes, she began to recite a calming mantra she learned in yoga classes at the gym. Om, Om, Ommmmmmmm. It didn't work.

When she opened her eyes, the crumbling fountain and cherubs were still there. The sight of the prayerful cherub with the partial face sent a chill over her. She jumped to her feet and walked briskly around the fountain three times to get her heart rate up. "This is ridiculous. I have to get it together," she said aloud. She couldn't admit that she'd lost it on a

Thursday morning jog in a familiar park. That type of thing didn't happen to someone her age. Her memory of time and place seemed distorted. Yesterday she'd been on the gravel path and it led to the iron bench where Angel sat. Yesterday the little pagoda sat where it always was—across the path close to the river. No pagoda in sight from where she stood now. The place she'd stumbled upon horrified her.

Alice wanted to run and never stop until she returned to her apartment. She didn't see the large piece of broken concrete on the path until she tripped and fell on all fours. Surprised and out of breath, she rolled herself down onto the ground and closed her eyes tightly to keep from crying. She wasn't sure how long she lay in a fetal position on the path by the fountain. The gravel began to dig into her arm on the ground and her knees felt stiff when she finally opened her eyes. She looked at her watch. An hour had passed since she left the apartment. As she sat up she saw the pagoda right in front of her—its metal roof wet with a heavy dew and large dewdrops sparkling on spider webs in its eaves. She turned to look across the path and there sat Angel on the antique bench peering at her with a quizzical look.

"I found you taking an early morning nap on the

grass. I didn't want to disturb you, my dear."

"I tripped. I wasn't napping. How long have you been watching me?"

"Not long. Enough time for you to get a good rest."

"Angel or whoever you are, I'm telling you I wasn't resting. I think I fainted after I tripped."

Alice stood up slowly and looked around in disbelief. No crumbling three cherub fountain, no circular path around the fountain, no dark beetles that looked like cigar stubs crawling in the leaf-strewn basin of the fountain. Confusion and panic overwhelmed her.

"Come, sit beside me, dear. I should have come to your aid, but I thought you were...never mind. You looked so peaceful there. You didn't seem injured in anyway. I must say, though, that you do seem rather out of sorts after your rest."

"Strange things are happening to me this morning. I found myself in a much older part of the park. I saw an old broken down fountain with three cherubs. Each one had different expressions on their faces. Well, actually, one did not have a whole face. I'm not making any sense, am I?" Alice felt dizzy and weak.

"Well, no, you aren't. Some days can be stranger than others."

"Well, Angel, it seems strange to me this is the fourth day you've been sitting here. Why are you always dressed the same every day? And why do you want to tell me a story about yourself? Where do you live? Who are you? Why is this part of the park different? How could I have missed the bench today? Where is the fountain I saw before I tripped? What does the pagoda mean? Why are we both here?"

The string of questions came from Alice's lips in staccato bursts. The questions seemed random and frantic, but she knew they were related to her experiences over the last three days. Her time with Angel had made her feel differently about her life, her education, her mother and Jeff, her whole purpose in being alive.

Angel seemed unperturbed by the questions. She adjusted her purple hat and fluffed her white curls. She looked down at her brown lace-up shoes, then straightened the purple and pink scarf around her neck. She reached to touch the upturned umbrella and rested her hand on the delicately carved handle. There were no leaves caught inside the canopy to brush away.

"You don't like my clothes? Oh my! Is that what you have been thinking about? You haven't thought about the stories, it seems. You haven't learned any lessons from my stories?"

"Yes, yes. I've been thinking about your stories." Alice felt ashamed that somehow she had offended Angel. Her demanding questions had been random and rude. *I haven't told her anything about myself, but I want to know all about her. She wants her stories to instruct me. I'm not learning what's important.*

As if she read Alice's thoughts Angel said, "I am ready to tell you another story. It is about a frog." Alice took a deep breath and sighed with contentment when Angel began the story.

20

DAY FOUR—THE STORY OF A FROG ANGEL

When I lived with my aunt in the city, I worked as a house servant for a very wealthy family. Well, yes, I left the farm. I had no intention tending cows the rest of my days and longed for other experiences. My aunt worked for the family many years as a cook. The mistress of the house happily hired me on her recommendation. As she fancied French manners, she insisted the servants call her Madame. She was not French. Why does it matter to you in what country my story took place? Doesn't matter to the story, at all. May I continue?

Though I wanted to work indoors, as inside maids were thought of more highly, my duties were in the gardens as well. Known as a farmer's daughter, it was a difficult time to escape others' views of what I could do. I became a helper in the flower gardens. Madame loved her gardens and spent much time there. She taught me how to train the sweet-smelling vines over the arbors. I was taller than most women and did not need a ladder like the gardener's young helper. The gardener instructed me how to plant seeds and bulbs. My responsibilities included gathering flowers and bringing them to the garden room where I arranged them in vases.

After I did the arrangements, Madame placed the vases about the house. The vases were all very expensive painted ones. Some had beautiful floral designs and a few were sparkling crystal. She taught me to use extreme care when arranging flowers, and only she carried the vases inside. Oh yes, my dear, the house was very large with many rooms.

She placed flower vases in the two parlors, the long dining room, the large library, and six bedrooms. I had been amazed when I learned there were so many bedrooms. Only Madame and her husband resided there year-round. Their two sons were students and lived at the University. Their nephew had an important role in the family, but I will explain about him later. As best I understood at the time, Madame's husband held an important position with the government as a financial minister. Servants were not told much about such things. In addition to my aunt, the servants included a cook's helper, a butler, another lad who helped the butler, a driver for the carriage, and two maids who were very lazy. They were all designated as house servants. I did other chores besides the flowers. I often went to post letters for her, shopped at the market, and mended Madame's clothes. My most enjoyable time was when I sat with Madame in the afternoons while she played the piano or wrote long letters to her sons at university. I met the sons briefly on three holiday occasions.

The nephew? You didn't forget I mentioned him. Younger? Why do you ask? I was younger than the nephew if you must know. Handsome? Some called him handsome. On with the story, please.

Most servants worked six days a week with Sunday off. On Saturday my aunt cooked enough for the family to have two hearty cold meals that the butler's helper served. My aunt did not work on Sunday, except during winter holiday season when Madame gave six dinner parties. The season of parties required extra servants who were hired from the town. Oh my, I am telling so much about the grand family that I have lost the thread of the story about the frog, haven't I?

You see, the frog was the gardener. His skill as a gardener pleased our employers, but two house servants called him a frog. The maid said he blinked slowly like a frog. The cook's helper said he stayed in the garden so much that he seemed like a creature who had always been there—like a frog in the pond. They said he often surprised other servants by appearing suddenly from behind a clump of trees or splashing about in the fountain. I believed he tended to his assigned chores. Everyone in the house began calling him Frog, instead of his true name, Gunter.

I spent many hours with Gunter learning about flowers and how to arrange colors in a pleasing manner. Gunter had talents that others did not know. He built lovely cabinets and painted them with pictures of all the flowers in the gardens. One day he invited me into the garden shed where in a corner he had constructed a small wood-working shop. Up until that time, he had not told anyone about the cabinets. I encouraged him to show the cabinets to Madame since she loved flowers and might pay him for one; yes, the cabinets were exquisite and well-made. He deserved to be paid for such beautiful work.

Why do you ask? Well, Gunter was older, much older than I. It is strange you keep inquiring about age. Oh, you are interested if I fell in love with him? My, my. You want to anticipate my story, but don't get ahead of me. You might be surprised.

Six months after I began work at the big house, Madame's nephew came to visit. The great flurry about the house surprised me. The lazy maids worked harder for an entire week as they cleaned and aired out the rooms, ironed linens, polished lamps, and so on. These were usual chores maids should do without complaint, except for the two lazy maids who constantly grumbled. And not only were they lazy, they often made fun of Gunter, laughing as they watched him hard at work in the flower gardens. I never spoke to those two girls unless required by Madame. When I did carry a message from Madame to one of them, they treated me with disrespect. They resented the fact that Madame assigned me varied chores and allowed me to sit in the parlor with her in the afternoons.

The nephew arrived on a Sunday while I attended a concert at the public hall with my aunt. I did not meet him for several days as he would leave early in the morning and often return late in the evening. The day I finally met him, he stood on the drive at the front of the house as I arrived at work. The carriage waited for him and the driver seemed impatient. He did strike me at the time as handsome. His name was Frederik with the same surname as Madame's husband—not blood kin to Madame, only her nephew by marriage. Not that that mattered to Madame. She said she loved him like she loved her own two sons. When he saw me, he bowed deeply and asked my name. His actions surprised me. Usually, gentlemen did not speak to the servants in such a manner. I stammered out something to him, slightly curtsied, and brushed past. He grabbed my arm and insisted that I speak clearly and tell him my name. When I told him my name was Arella, he exclaimed, "How enchanting." He said my name sounded like a melody on wings. I felt extremely uncomfortable with his remark and asked if I could please go inside. His carriage waited for him and I wanted to report for the day to Madame.

Yes, yes, dear, the encounter made me very uneasy.

Frederik smiled at me and told me that we could become acquainted at dinner that evening. He then jumped into the carriage and ordered the driver to be off to wherever he went for the day. I knew he had been wrong about having dinner with me that evening. Servants never dined with the family. Evidently, he mistook me for Madame's friend. Society was different then. Strict class division kept servants in their place. You have never experienced class divisions like we did in the old country. Madame must not have made it clear to Frederik that I was a servant.

However, Frederik often was close by when I arranged flowers or left the house to collect the post. He began conversations by complimenting me on my hair or commenting on the weather. Once he plucked a flower from a flower arrangement with a flourish and presented it to me. Stammering and blushing, I accepted the flower but immediately put it back into the vase.

One day I grew suspicious when I saw him with another gentleman at the back of the garden. I observed the person had not entered the garden from the house but from a back gate that led to the street. Over the next several weeks, Frederik and the unknown man talked earnestly by the back gate. I never saw the person's face because he always wore a brown hat pulled low over his eyes. The conversations happened during the afternoon time when Madame went to tea with friends. I thought I was the only person who observed the mysterious encounters. Afraid to tell my mistress about her beloved nephew's actions, I finally went to Gunter's garden workshop one day to confide in him. I asked his advice about whether I should mention to Madame these secretive meetings between her nephew and a stranger.

Oh dear, yes, yes. I was very shy; but Gunter, even though they called him Frog, was always kind to me. In those days a female house servant did not strike up a conversation with a man. Well, yes, we were both servants, but I worked inside and he worked outside the house. It is hard to understand, but try. Working class, you said. We did not use that phrase. You are very interested in this class business, I must say. To continue, my dear, Gunter assured me that I made the right decision to confide in him. Yet, he did not advise me what I should do about the nephew's suspicious actions.

About a week later, a terrible thing happened at the house. Madame and her husband left to visit friends in the country. Frederik left with them. My aunt and I were at her small home nearby. We were the only two house servants who did not live on the grounds. Everyone but Gunter had been given a holiday for two days. He stayed behind as he wanted to prune the large oak trees while the others were gone.

Sometime over the next days, a thief broke into the house and many valuable items were taken, including Madame's collection of fine jewelry and several priceless vases. Naturally, when the robbery was discovered upon our employer's return, their suspicions fell on Gunter. Madame and her husband summoned Gunter into the parlor and questioned him.

Two black uniformed policemen arrived later the same day and spoke with Gunter at length. All the servants gathered to watch and listen. The officers accused Gunter of knowledge of the robbery. Gunter said he had no information and that nothing had seemed amiss. For his only pleasure he admitted he occasionally went to the nearby tavern. That's where he went the first evening after everyone departed. Other than one absence, he stated he'd been busy with trimming the trees. It escaped his notice that the door from the garden to the main house had been forced open and left slightly damaged by the thief. Proof of his industrious trimming was evident since all the trees in the garden were pruned to perfection and stacks of tree limbs lay in piles under the trees.

Gunter was stunned he had been accused since

he had been a faithful employee for ten years. To the surprise of all the servants, Frederik made several comments to the police about Gunter's untrustworthiness and that he should not have been left on the premises alone. All the servants talked among themselves speculating about Frog's guilt. I determined to help prove Gunter's innocence, but I did not know how.

A few days later as I gathered the last summer flowers, I started into the house and saw Frederik enter Gunter's gardening shed. He carried something in his hands, but I could not tell what. He went in and out very quickly, looking around to see if anyone observed him. I stood in the shadows of the room where I arranged the flowers and he could not see me; then, he went out the back garden gate that led to the street.

In a few hours, a policeman rang the loud bell at the front door. I sat with Madame in the parlor helping her write down an inventory of the remaining vases. Six in all were stolen, including three of her favorites. The policeman said he came back to search the garden area to see if any evidence could be found. I wanted to tell Madame about watching Frederik in the garden, but fear kept me silent.

My dear, my dear, servants had reasons not to

tell their employer everything. Often servants were not deemed honest until they proved themselves over many years. Employers were wary of the working class, as you like to call servants. Well, that's just the way society ran in those days. And I am sure you can guess what happened when the policeman searched the garden area. Yes, yes, some stories follow a certain pattern, I know. Am I boring you?

The policeman searched the grounds and the gardener's shed. Of course, the officer found the supposed proof of Gunter's guilt in one of the drawers of a cabinet, the one with the painted flowers. A piece of Madame's jewelry wrapped in a man's brown hat lay inside one of the missing vases which had been roughly bound in burlap. The policeman immediately took Gunter away and placed him in the city jail.

Now I ask you—would any servant be so stupid as to do such a thing—leave items stolen from his employer in a shed on his employer's property?

Madame wept bitterly that her trusted gardener would commit such a deed. When Frederik returned late that afternoon and heard the news about Gunter's arrest, he seemed very satisfied. He boasted to Madame that his suspicions were correct about the gardener's guilt, no mistake about it. Frederik said this to her when the butler and I were in the parlor trying to calm Madame.

I couldn't keep silent any longer. I knew about Frederik's meetings in the back of the garden with a man in a brown hat. I hoped Gunter had seen the man with Frederik, too. Gathering all my courage, I told Madame that I did not believe Gunter capable of being a thief. She always said she trusted me and thought me an honest girl. Why would I lie to her? Pointing my finger at Frederik I told her that she should ask him about the man in the garden, a man in a brown hat exactly like the one found in Gunter's cabinet.

Of course, my accusation shocked Madame. Frederik had his back to us, but I could tell he seethed with rage. "How dare a servant accuse me? I know nothing about a person in a brown hat!" he shouted and ran from the parlor. He slammed the heavy carved door so violently that an untidy stack of books fell from the bookshelf. Madame looked at me in distress and fell weeping onto a large sofa. I pleaded with her to bring Gunter home and question him about Frederik and the man in a brown hat. She told me that she would try but she felt that the matter might be out of her hands now that Gunter was under arrest. She said she did think it odd when the jewelry and vase were found in his shed. Somehow I knew that she believed me, not Frederik.

This story does have a somewhat happy ending. Frog, I mean Gunter, was, of course, innocent. Madame went the next day to the police station and made a surprising revelation. With her husband by her side, she told the authorities that Frederik demanded money from her to pay his gambling debts. She'd provided cash to him many times, but always without her husband's knowledge. He'd threatened to tell his uncle vicious lies about her if she did not continue to pay his debts. His threats had frightened her. She believed him capable of planning a robbery and blaming someone else. Everyone would believe him, the beloved nephew, not the lowly gardener called Frog. She asked for Gunter to be set free. With her statement, the authorities released Gunter. The police promised they would promptly go to the house and question Frederik.

You can imagine my admiration of a woman who would tell the truth about her own weakness to save her gardener a prison term. By the time the authorities returned to the house to confront Frederik, he had fled in haste taking several more of Madame's priceless vases with him. Charges against Frederik were never brought by his aunt and uncle.

If the story circulated about Madame's admission to the police and her accusation against Frederik, there would have been a great scandal. The family received news several months later that Frederik drowned at sea off the coast of Africa. Madame never spoke of him again.

Gunter was never called Frog again. I continued with my work as a maid for several years until I found a more suitable position. Gunter continued as the family's head gardener until just after his seventy-eighth birthday. They found him dead of a heart attack in his garden shed, paint brush in hand and a partially decorated flower cabinet nearby. In later years he sold many beautiful painted cabinets and left most of the heavy gardening work to a younger helper. He lived a long full life and did the things he loved.

**

Alice's face clouded with dismay.

"You look surprised with the end of the story," said Angel.

"It is not what I expected."

"A good storyteller keeps the listener wondering how a story will end, don't you agree?"

"I thought the story would be about a frog—the animal—a real frog. Instead, you told about a man called Frog. Your stories are never what they should be."

"Remember, my dear, the servants mockingly called him Frog. His true name was Gunter. You made a strange remark. Why did you say a story should be a certain thing? You can't tell what a story should be, only what it is, Alice."

"Are these stories really about you? I hoped to hear you fell in love with Gunter."

"Humph...why would you wish that to be the story?"

"Well, that's the way fairy tales usually end. You know, a certain expected ending."

Angel did not answer, but gave her usual signal that storytelling time was over. She reached for her umbrella and snapped it shut, but only after brushing away a few yellow leaves. The trees were beginning to show fall color in the park. In a few weeks, the deciduous trees would be bare, leaving only the stately dark firs and spruces showing a dusky grey-greens for the rest of the winder. Alice wondered if Angel would come to the park every day during the colder months. Alice jogged every month of the year except for January when early mornings were extremely cold. Time to leave for today, so she reached down to pull the shoestrings of her running shoes tighter.

"Good day, Alice. Enjoy your exercise," said Angel, ending her silence.

"Thank you for the story even though it wasn't what I expected."

"Life and good stories are never what you expect."

"Will I see you tomorrow? It's Friday, last day of classes."

"It is likely I will be here again," Angel nodded as she spoke.

Alice walked slowly away from Angel who still sat on the bench, umbrella in hand. She began to pick up her pace and ran with a sense of well-being that she hadn't felt in several weeks. She never looked back to see if Angel still sat on the bench surrounded by bright yellow leaves at her feet.

21

DAY FOUR—THURSDAY

BEA

On Thursday Bea usually went to the market in the morning and took Sweetie to the park in the late afternoon. Bea knew Sweetie did not like Thursdays—she could tell by the way he whined when she left. Her regular shopping took from eleven until one o'clock so she didn't often get to the park until about three. However, this Thursday Bea changed her rigid schedule. She tried to convince herself that the market was too crowded at eleven. She actually wanted to be in the park at the same time as the previous three days. Bea hoped Bounty would again be at the bench, but that the pigeons would not be there. It annoyed her the way the birds pecked around the ground, flapped their wings, and waited for the handouts of food. With endless patience, Bounty tossed handfuls of crumbs to them before and after each story. She always left a small amount in the bag. When Bea asked her why she didn't use all the crumbs each day, she cocked her head at Bea and said, "I don't want the bread to run out. There should be left-overs to start another day, you know." Answers like that from Bounty puzzled Bea.

She was determined that today she would ask questions that Bounty would have to answer straight. She wanted to know Bounty's home country and why she always dressed in white. Most of all, Bea planned to ask about the strange building, the pagoda. Bea hadn't seen such old-fashioned structures like it in the main park. And why didn't the city pave that rough gravel path, anyway? All other paths were the same—smooth and even blacktop, easy to walk. Of course, she didn't like the fact that the blacktop also meant bicyclists whizzed by pedestrians. Sweetie startled easily and Bea worried that he might leap into the path of an oncoming bike and be injured. *Such a small dog might not be seen. What a disaster that would be for everyone involved.* Bea worried and fumed about the possibility of bad things happening, accidents she could not prevent, people being rude in lines, or not finding items she wanted at the market.

Life for Bea was a series of possible frustrations. She knew her former co-workers called her the grumpiest woman alive, but she didn't care. She found plenty of reasons in the world to be grumpy. Yet, she'd felt hopeful when she listened to Bounty's stories the last three days—hope for her was a most unfamiliar feeling. Besides, she rather enjoyed the fanciful stories even if she puzzled over them.

As she walked, Bea thought she somehow had forgotten how far it was to the small gravel path. Sweetie seemed to be confused, too. He ran a little ahead on the loose leash and then back trying to locate the path. Finally, a few minutes later, she did see a path but as she walked she felt a sense of apprehension. Now the low walls weren't covered with vines as before. She saw only a faint outline of the pagoda far up ahead. Perhaps the light is different today, she thought. The bench was not in sight. Bea walked steadily but she never seemed to be closer to the pagoda.

Sweetie began to tire and needed to stop for a pee on the grass. Bea impatiently waited for the canine business to conclude and then continued on, walking even faster so that Sweetie's little legs pumped furiously to keep up with the pace. Bea looked at her watch and realized that today she had walked much longer than yesterday. She worried she was on a wrong path. Even the gravel under her feet seemed different. Instead of a light sandy beige path she remembered, a darker coarse gravel crunched loudly with each step she took. As she looked toward the river to get her bearings, she realized she could no longer see the outline of the pagoda; but, instead, she saw a crumbling fountain encircled by stepping stones.

"We took a wrong turn, Sweetie. How did that happen?" Bea said aloud. Sweetie didn't answer, of course, just looked at Bea and perked one ear.

"Let's sit on the side of the fountain and rest. Then we'll go back. I must be confused."

Again, Sweetie didn't answer but perked the other ear as if to say he understood. Dogs, even very spoiled and ill-tempered ones, know when their owner is agitated.

The fountain presented a sad sight. Two of the walls surrounding the basin were broken. Chunks of plaster peeled off all sides. Bea chose carefully a place to sit on the deteriorated walls. Three figures of small children were at the center portion of the fountain. As Bea sat warily on the most stable side of the fountain, she felt even more uneasy. The three figures in the fountain disturbed her. The faces of the small statues were smashed away, but the bodies were intact. *Why would anyone do such a thing? Juvenile delinquents, for sure. Why is this wreck of a fountain still standing? The usual city problem of not maintaining what they built.* Bea had a terrible opinion of almost anything the city did, including the way they carelessly swept the streets and made rules to force citizens to recycle newspapers and plastics.

Bea heaved a large sigh, stood up, and told Sweetie to heel. She wanted to find her way back to the other part of the park. It seemed ridiculous that she missed the right path. Anger and apprehension flared inside her, and she didn't see the large fallen tree branch on the path. As she stumbled over the branch, Sweetie's leash came out of her hand. She fell to her knees and saw Sweetie run away with the leash trailing on the gravel path.

"Oh no, oh no. Sweetie, come. Sweetie, come," Bea cried after her escaping pet. Sweetie kept running until she lost sight of him around a curve in the path. Bea felt faint and tried to rise. She thought that perhaps she should rest briefly to recover. In a moment, she'd need to get up and find her disobedient dog; then she closed her eyes and felt the sun on her face.

"Señora, señora, how long have you been here?" Bea stirred but did not open her eyes. She heard a soft voice that urgently whispered to her.

The voice spoke louder. "I found your little pet running loose."

Bea's eyes opened and she saw that Bounty stood by the old iron bench with Sweetie sitting patiently beside her. *Where was she? How did she get to the bench? What happened?* Bea pulled herself to her feet, angrily brushing herself off.

"I fell on the path and Sweetie ran off."

"Sweetie came right to me like a good dog when I called him."

"Sweetie never goes to other people." Bea stuck her finger in front of Sweetie's little fuzzy face and said, "Bad dog! Bad dog!"

Bea started to tell Bounty about her confusion and how she seemed lost, but here was the bench and her dog Sweetie. She looked across the path and saw the old sad pagoda. *Did I hallucinate?* She did not know what to tell Bounty. She didn't want to say she fell over a tree branch after she saw a forlorn dry fountain. *Such things don't usually happen to me. There's no explanation. No fountain with faceless kids in sight. What on earth does this mean?*

"I fell down. I scrapped my shin and my ankle hurts. Injuries at my age are only a nuisance. You know, it's useless to see a doctor unless you're dying."

"Please sit on the bench, Bea. You have not had a good morning so far. There, see how nice Sweetie sits by me? Oh, look, he wants to go under the bench to sleep. He will stay there and you can rest. I'll begin another story for you. Maybe a long one today?" Bea shrugged. She wanted to ask Bounty the questions she had planned. "Thank you," she said, instead. "Yes, please do entertain me with a story again."

"Entertain? You mean like something not real or something funny? That's not what my stories are about."

"I'm trying to puzzle out what your stories mean."

"Good for you. Now I'll begin the next story for you," said Bounty.

22

DAY FOUR—THE STORY OF A FROG BOUNTY

My mamá left her cousin's chicken farm and found work in the city. Her dead papá's second cousin worked at a great house for a banker's family. Cousin Maria was a teacher for the only child of the family. *Si*, bankers were the same then as now—made rich from the people. Of course, Maria came from a poor family, but she had teacher's education. She earned good pay and helped her family. She taught the banker's son who had problems with French language. The family only spoke that language to him. He could speak Spanish easily but stumbled over French words his parents wanted him to know. I don't know if the banker was a Frenchman or not. It might matter to the story if you listen now instead of asking so many questions. The wife of the banker told Maria to call her Madame, which was French. A woman in that country would be called *Señora*, not Madame.

Cousin Maria recommended my mamá to her employer. She was hired to be the old cook's helper and trained to prepare favorite family dishes. My mamá didn't know about cooking, but she proved a quick learner. She learned about chickens and she learned about cooking, too. Mamá lived with Maria in a little house next to the big house.

Well, the big house wasn't *una hacienda.* Those were outside the city and were like a Western ranch on TV. This big house was *muy grande.*

Mamá learned very quickly how to prepare dishes the family liked. Madame ordered special tins of different foods that arrived on the boats once a month. The head cook kept everything locked in kitchen cabinet—the special supplies could only be used for the family's meal, never for servants. Madame checked once a week and would tell my mamá to keep list of what should be ordered. There were boxes of skinny cookies, dried fruits my mamá had never seen, little tins of tiny black fish eggs, and small bags of herbs. Madame also ordered a special flour to make little pancakes for her son.

Many servants worked for Madame and her rich husband. A man who served as driver and guard for the banker lived in the house to keep the banker safe. The ones who worked at the house lived close by in the neighborhood where other servants of rich families lived. There were two sister maids who were very lazy. A gardener and his simple minded son lived in a small room close to the big garage where the banker's large black automobile was kept. The young son had a different look about him. His large bulging eyes blinked slowly when he was told what to do by his papá, the gardener. The lazy sister maids, who often smoked in the garden when they should have been working, had seen him hopping happily in the garden around the little pond full of large golden fishes. The two maids laughed at the simple boy when he played in the garden. They said his name should be Frog. Soon everyone else in the house began calling him by that name, too, even Madame. His real name was Flavio—that means yellow hair. A simple yellow-haired boy, he didn't have the mind for practical things. He'd never gone to school but always worked with his papá in the garden since he was very small. No one knew anything about his mother.

One day, about a month after my mamá began

her work as cook's helper, the servants were called together and told they would soon have an important visitor. The beloved nephew of the banker would soon arrive by ship. He would stay for the whole winter season. Of course, winter in that country wasn't a season of cold weather. The city was close to sea and jungle with nice pleasant winters. The son of the family was very happy to hear that another person would be in the house. He wanted a friend. He was lonely as only child.

Of course, the son was not allowed to have Flavio as a companion. That was not the way. Flavio, a simple son of the gardener, couldn't be *compadre* to banker's son. Don't you know that's the way it is between masters and servants? No mixing with the servants. You must not have learned your own family's history in this country. You don't know your family history? How strange. Maybe we could talk about that after the story is over. Please, I'll continue.

The nephew arrived on the big boat on Sunday morning, and the family had a grand party to welcome him. Many of the bankers' friends and wives attended. My mamá and the cook prepared the family's favorite dishes for three days. The servants got only few glimpses of the nephew during the first days after his arrival. He stayed most of the day in his rooms, resting from the long sea voyage. They heard from the neighbors that Nephew left early each evening and often did not return until very late at night, causing all the guard dogs in yards of the big houses to bark. It was what they were trained to do.

Madame seemed very happy to have him in the house, but the son was disappointed that Nephew hadn't paid attention to him. Mamá knew this because Maria, his tutor, had told Mamá about the son's feelings. They had a special bond of student and teacher. Madame was usually too busy to pay much attention to her child, which seemed not natural to Maria and Mamá.

A month after the nephew arrived, the air in the house changed. The lazy sister maids gossiped to other servants about Nephew's attention to Maria and my mamá. He often stopped one of them in the hallways between the kitchens or outside in gardens. He would only approach one when the other wasn't present, but the maids saw what happened. Mamá overheard what was said by the gossiping maids. They implied that mamá and her cousin encouraged his advances. It was lies. He would seek out each of them almost daily, compliment them, and ask them to meet him after work at a nearby tavern. He said he would introduce them to his companions. He bragged he had many drinking and gambling friends who would welcome two beautiful women to join them. Mamá and Maria told him they were not that kind of women. No one ever said they heard Mamá and Marie refuse him. The servants were very cruel to talk the way they did.

One day when the gardener saw the banker's nephew trying to push Mamá into the flower-covered arbor in the garden, he walked up with very large hoe in his hand and told him to leave the cook's helper alone or he would tell Madame. The nephew laughed at him and said that Madame would not believe a gardener's tales, but he never bothered my mamá again after that day. Flavio, the yellow-haired son called Frog, was also there and watched his papá help Mamá. She thanked the gardener for his help, but of course, she did not mention what had happened for fear she would be scorned. She was afraid to report the bad actions of the beloved nephew of the family. No one would believe her. She was only the cook's helper and had not worked there long enough to prove her honesty.

A month later the terrible thing happened. The family, including Nephew, had gone *a la hacienda* for big family celebration. It was time of winter *fiesta* for whole city. All the servants had been given two days off to celebrate patron saint with their families. No, I don't remember name of saint . It doesn't matter. The story could be told in any place, remember that. You have never been to a *fiesta* of a patron saint? Dancing and music and also *muchos bebidos* drinking. Children set off fireworks and old men tell stories. You've missed many things by being such a sour person. Are you angry at me for saying that? I speak as your friend. You should try to be a happy person. Look at me. I feed pigeons and tell you stories, two things that make me happy every day. Now, I want to continue with my story.

The gardener and his son called Frog were the only ones at the house and they must have been sleeping in their room when it happened. A bad person broke into the side door that faced the street. Madame's jewels were stolen along with important papers belonging to her husband, the banker. When the family returned and found they had been robbed, they suspected the gardener and his son.

But why, I would ask, would the gardener stay if he had stolen from the house? They would have run away and sold the jewels, no? The lazy maids said the boy called Frog might steal because he was so simple. This made no sense as Flavio did not know about the jewels since he had never been allowed inside the house. There were many questions about the robbery that could not be answered.

The policemen, who came after the banker reported the robbery, were also convinced that the simple boy might have seen or even helped the thief enter the house while his papá was asleep. The officers took Flavio and his papá down to the police station for more questions. After *siesta*, the two returned from the station looking very tired from answering all the questions. They did not know anything and had not been helpful to the police. The police let them go but said their investigation would continue. The banker stormed about the house and shouted that the police must catch the person who robbed him.

The next day as my mamá picked garden herbs, she saw the nephew sneak into gardener's rooms. The gardener and his son had gone to buy new bricks to repair broken ones on the pathway around the garden. Mamá could tell by the way he looked around many times before entering the shed that the nephew did not want to be seen. It wasn't a surprise to Mamá when the policeman returned in a short time and told Madame they wanted to search the grounds for any traces the thieves may have left. Of course, they went straight to the gardener's rooms and began throwing things out of the cupboards and from the shelves. Hidden under Flavio's mattress was a small bundle and inside were two of Madame's emerald earrings that had been a wedding present from her mother-in-law.

Now, tell me, do you think a gardener would be so stupid and hide stolen jewels under the mattress of his own simple son? He was an honest man. Mamá knew that the nephew had put the jewels there so the gardener would be arrested for robbing his employer. All the servants and Madame gathered in the garden to watch the police arrest the gardener.

Frog, I mean Flavio, wailed as two policemen began to lead his papá away. He hardly ever spoke, but he began to speak about shouts and cries he'd heard several days before. He had heard arguments while sitting under the windows of Madame's bedroom as he played with the black and white cat that sometimes came into the garden. He was scared by the angry voices he heard coming from the bedroom window and ran to tell his papá.

"Tell what I heard. Papá, tell what I heard. I told you. Yelling. Mad voices. Madame's voice. Man's voice." It was the most words anyone had ever heard from Frog's mouth. Would anyone believe his strange words?

Cousin Maria stepped forward and asked if she could speak before the police took the gardener away. Madame looked at her in amazement because Maria had spoken so boldly. She was known for being very quiet and shy except when teaching lessons to the son. Her voice was loud and strong when she spoke to the police.

"I teach French and Spanish to Madame's son. The words that Frog heard were French. He asked me the meaning of one word he heard. It was word for money. The man's voice kept shouting about *argent.* He told me Madame cried loudly every time the man shouted that word. I think Madame and her nephew were arguing about money. You should question her nephew."

The policemen appeared very confused about Maria's statements. He said Madame's nephew came to the station that morning and accused the gardener of the robbery. The nephew suggested the police search more carefully the premises around the garden. He gave them permission to search the gardener's rooms. Since he was the banker's nephew, the policeman assumed he was a dutiful relative eager to help solve the crime.

Madame suddenly looked very unwell and said

she was going into the house to get out of the bright sun. She said she would bring the nephew out to speak with the police. The servants, the officers, and the gardener waited in silence for several long minutes. Suddenly, they heard the noise of an automobile engine and tire wheels that screeched on the pavement. The policemen ran to the front of the house in time to see that Madame had fled with her husband's nephew. They drove away together in the banker's black car. The car roared away down the long boulevard. Not knowing what to make of this, the officer in charge released the gardener and informed the astounded servants that they would make a report to their captain. They would contact the banker immediately about the sudden flight of his wife and his nephew. Yes, yes, this does begin to sound like one of your soaps, doesn't it? The soaps or *telenovelas* were very popular in the country where my mamá was born. Oh, you think you can now tell me the ending of the story? Please, let me hear.

**

Now the roles were reversed. Bea told the story to Bounty. Bea was familiar with this type of story because she watched the soaps every afternoon.

Bea felt the words flow from her.

"The madame and the nephew were lovers and always spoke French to each other. The nephew needed money to pay people who threatened him over his gambling debts. They argued about how to get the money since the banker was very strict with funds and allowed Madame only a small amount of cash. What he gave her was only enough to run the house and pay the servants each week. The two decided if the nephew hired two of his companions to steal Madame's jewelry, they could pay his debts with the sale of the stolen jewels and run away together. Someone had to take the blame for the robbery so they choose the gardener. Flavio, the boy called Frog, had little to do with the whole matter except for reporting the argument he overheard. How's that for an ending the soaps would have?"

Bea was out of breath after telling her version of the story's end. Bounty looked very satisfied with the ending of the story from Bea.

"Wonderful. Wonderful. You are good at telling stories, too."

"Why did you tell me it was a story about a frog? The only use of the word frog was the name of the simple boy in your story. That's not right," said Bea.

"What is right about a story? A good storyteller can use the word in any way, don't you think?"

Bounty began gathering up the sacks of left-over bread crumbs. Sweetie awoke from the nap he had been taking under the bench during the storytelling. Bea knew it was time to leave once again and return to the apartment and have a late lunch. As she walked away she pondered the whole story about Frog. *People are often not what they seem. Maybe I'm always too quick to judge.* She felt pleased that she had finished the story for Bounty.

23

DAY FOUR—THURSDAY

CAROL

Carol dreaded school on Thursdays. Math homework was due. Last night she struggled for the solutions and asked for help several times; however, her mom had told Carol to work them out herself. Every evening since Monday her mom poured over ads in the papers for apartments or talked on the phone with friends. Carol worked the problems as best she could but successfully completed only half. Again, like each night during the past week, Carol went to bed with a stomach ache. In addition, she had begun a nervous habit of scratching her scalp at bedtime. After several days she felt like her head was on fire. She knew it was a bad habit, but she kept doing it until she fell asleep.

Once at school Carol tried not to worry about fourth period math class. Her friend Celeste sympathized with her and wanted to help, but lunch time was too short to work on math problems. Celeste suggested Carol ask their teacher, Mr. Padilla, for a tutor who could help her in the future. That would be the logical thing to do, but Carol knew that tutors cost money. Her mom had made it very clear that there was no cash for anything extra until they could get settled in a new place. They were on a very tight budget.

When the unfinished math assignment was turned in, Carol felt relieved. If she received the grade she thought she deserved on the homework assignment, it could mean a failing grade for the period. Yet, she didn't care about failing math. All she could really think about was school's end. She wanted to go back to the park and talk to Charity again. Carol had always wished for a big sister and Charity filled that longing. If she and her mom had to move farther from the park she could still walk there or catch the city bus. *It's a good idea for me to learn the bus schedules. I could get to the park by myself.* Carol desperately wanted to continue her after school time with Charity. *I don't need to tell Mom about Charity and the stories yet. I won't tell until things are settled.*

When last bell rang, Carol raced out of P.S. 236 to the park. She double checked her backpack for her sketch pad. *Maybe today Charity would pose for the portrait.* Carol walked faster than usual to reach the gravel path. The faster she walked the more excited she became. She thought her pace would surely get her there quickly, but the path was not in sight. Time seemed to race by and still she could not see the turn. She stopped by a row of bushes with dried late summer roses that clung stubbornly to the stems. She felt uneasy about where she stood in the park. The surroundings did not seem as familiar as yesterday. Turning around, she stood in the middle of the paved path and looked back. *Oh, there it is! How could I have missed the little path?* As she made the turn onto the gravel, she still felt unsettled.

The path looked different today. It was narrow and the stone walls along the sides were broken down. She remembered the walls had been covered with dark green vines. Now all the vines were brown and withered. Walking more slowly, Carol tried to spot the pagoda up ahead but giant evergreen trees overshadowed the path. When she came out of the shadows of the trees she saw an old fountain where she thought the pagoda should have been. She stopped so abruptly that the backpack fell off her shoulder. There wasn't a bench in sight. A sense of panic rose in her heart. She must have gone down the wrong path. She hadn't been in this spot the last three afternoons. She'd been in a pleasant old-fashioned part of the park that made her feel safe. The place where she stood bewildered her. The river was on her left but the river looked still and dark, no little rippling waves, and no boats in sight. She bent to pick up her backpack on the ground and noticed some little stepping stones that led to the fountain. *I'll look at the fountain and then go back and find the right path, the one to the bench and the pagoda.* "Charity will be there," she repeated three times out loud to give herself courage.

As Carol approached the fountain she fought back her fears and became more curious. In the middle of the fountain were three figures of little kids. Then she remembered photos her art teacher had shown of old buildings in Europe. On those buildings were carved figures just like these in different poses. The three figures were little baby angels all holding hands. Their faces were upturned to the sky. One of the angels smiled, one had a look of surprise, and the other prayed with eyes shut. All of the faces looked faded by the weather but were pretty. Carol took the sketch book out of the backpack and sat on a low wall of the fountain and began to furiously draw the figures. She felt inspired to draw each figure exactly as she saw them, weather-worn but beautiful. It would be a great addition to her growing collection of black and white sketches of objects in the park. Her teacher had called her work a portfolio, a nice adult word for an art project. The drawings took her twenty minutes of intense concentration. Her pencil flew with graceful strokes that caught the outlines of the figures and the expressions on the baby angel faces. Only once did she stop to erase a line or two.

When she finished she let out a big breath. She hastily tucked the sketchbook into the side pocket of the backpack. She felt dizzy and she realized she must have held her breath part of the time while she worked on the sketch. When she was a little kid she would have tantrums and hold her breath until she fainted. All of a sudden that's how she felt, like she would faint. She slid off the wall to sit on the ground and put her head between her knees. That's what Mr. Padilla had told her to do one day when she felt this way at school after a very hard math test. She sat with her eyes closed and counted to one hundred. She counted very, very slowly and took slow deep breaths. She didn't remember reaching one hundred.

"Hey, kid! Why are you sitting on the ground like that?"

Carol's head jerked up. Charity stood over her. Carol realized she leaned against the back of the iron bench, her legs almost covered by bright orange and yellow leaves.

"What? I was at the fountain."

"The fountain? Nooooo. You were sitting right there when I got here. What were you doing anyway?"

Carol stood up and saw the red backpack lying on the bench.

"How did my backpack get on the bench?"

"Duh, you must have put it there." Charity laughed.

"I hate it when someone says "duh." It means the other person is stupid."

"Hey, sorry, I wasn't calling you stupid. But next time, sit on the bench, not in the bushes behind it, OK? It looked a little crazy."

"Don't call me crazy either! What happened to me was weird." Carol spoke softly.

"So what happened to you?'

"Well, I missed the path and found an old fountain with little angels in it."

"Carol, that is very weird and crazy. Why were angels in a fountain?"

"You don't believe me, do you? The angels were statues in the middle of the old fountain and I drew them."

"Really? You drew a picture of some baby angels in the middle of a very old fountain...huh. It was here in the park, right?"

"I'll show you!"

Carol pulled the book from the side pocket of the backpack and opened it. On the page was the detailed sketch of three little chubby angels holding hands.

"Wow. Nice picture. Looks kinda familiar. What are they looking at?"

"At the sky. See, one is smiling, one looks surprised, and the other one..." Carol stopped when she saw the look on Charity's face.

"Yeah, and the last one looks like she is praying. Well, kid, I am impressed with your talent."

"Don't call me kid!"

"Oh, come on," Charity laughed. "You had an inspiration to draw angels. Good for you."

"It wasn't inspiration. They were real." Carol's

eyes filled with big tears.

"Hey, let me tell you another story for now and we can talk about angels later."

"Seems pointless." Carol's voice sounded flat.

"What do you mean pointless?"

"You've told me a story three days in a row. You say I've had an inspiration. Now you want to tell me another story. Seems pointless to me to hear another story about your grandmother."

"My grandmother was a very wonderful grandmother. She taught me a lot."

"So you are trying to teach me what your grandmother taught you. OK, OK. Now I think I get it. You are teaching me, poor kid, who doesn't have a grandmother. And...I don't have a brother or sister, either."

"I'm sorry. I know that must be awful for you."

"Don't feel sorry for me. I have my mom." Carol's comment was stubbornly defensive.

"I don't feel sorry for you. I know you are lonely and don't want to move away from your apartment." Charity seemed really serious for once.

"What did you say about my moving away?" Carol was stunned by the remark. She didn't remember telling Charity about the plans to move. How could she know that? She looked at the concern on

Charity's face. She didn't want to continue talking about moving away, or angels, or a fountain, or a change in her life.

"Never mind. Go on. Tell me another story so we don't have to talk about sad old fountains or other weird stuff happening to me. I want to listen, not talk."

"I understand. This one's about a frog and you won't be able to guess the ending."

Charity began another story.

24

DAY FOUR—THE STORY OF A FROG

CHARITY

My grandmother Spring Peach left the pig farm. Oops, I forgot. You like her Chinese name. Begin again. My grandmother Chun Tao left the pig farm and went to the city to find a better job and a husband. Girls married while they were still young and were expected to have lots of babies, especially boys. The custom was that the family would pick the man the girl should marry. A person called a matchmaker helped families find men for their daughters to marry. The girls did not have much to say about it. Really sucks, huh? Why do I use that term? You know what that means. Kids in your class must say it all the time. Well, probably my grandmother did not say "it sucks" but something close to it if she had been forced to marry someone she did not know. Let's keep going with the real story. She told me when I lived with her that she didn't really want just any man for a husband, especially she did not want to marry a pig farmer like her cousin.

She found a small room to rent with the money she had saved from the job at the pig farm. Sure, she probably still had the valuable urns or maybe not. I don't know how long this story was after the pigs died and she found the treasure. Grandmother got things mixed up when she was old. Time meant nothing to her. What's that? What's it like to live with an old person? Really nice because she told me stories like I am trying to tell you. Zip it for now! You said you wanted to listen. You're questioning me like the cops on TV.

Chun Tao, my grandmother, walked around the city to see all the shops and what people did in the shops. There were shops where people sewed, shops with meat hanging in the windows—yuck, again—shops that sold bowls of noodles, shops with bowls and pans for sale, shops that were dark and smelled bad, shops where women were standing by the door and invited men to come in. She didn't want to do any of those jobs so she didn't ever ask about being hired in the shops in the middle of the city. She heard from an old woman who sold flowers on the street that rich families in large compounds hired young girls to sweep the courtyards and do other work inside the house. A woman at a noodle shop told her the name of the street where the big houses were located. Grandmother walked for a long time to find the street. She stopped and asked several other people on the way. The street she found was wider than the ones in the part of the city with the shops. All of the houses had tall walls around them and heavy wooden gates. There were fierce guard dogs chained outside the gates of the compounds. It seemed that the people inside the walls were very afraid of strangers who might come to the gates. Hey, it really doesn't affect the story for me to tell you the kind of dogs they were. Dogs, mean barking dogs. Grandmother didn't know the kind of dogs. You can ask so many questions, Carol. I know you never talk this much at school. How about listening now?

Grandmother told me what happened was most fortunate for her. She heard shouts from behind one of the gates; suddenly, the heavy door swung open. A young girl was pushed out onto the street by a very angry older woman. "Get out, get out, you lazy girl. Anyone off the street could do a better job than you. I know you stole from Master. Here! Take the coins and leave. Get out, get out." The woman threw a handful of coins onto the street. Coins rolled down the street and the girl who had been thrown out bent to pick them up and then ran away. The angry woman looked at my grandmother and shouted to her. "You can do a better job than that lazy girl I am sure. Come here, come here. Tell me the province where your family lives."

That is how my grandmother was hired to work in the big house owned by a wealthy middle-aged landowner and his very young beautiful wife. She was really the second wife, but that's another long story. The angry woman who hired my grandmother was in charge of all the servants that worked inside the house. She came from the same province as my grandmother. The woman questioned my grandmother for a long time until she was convinced of her honesty and her willingness to work.

The woman's name was Dongmei. I was going to tell you what her name meant. It translates to Winter Plum. Pretty funny, huh, Spring Peach hired by Winter Plum. The other servants in the house were an old man who had been with the family for many years, a fat cook and her skinny helper. Another young girl, mute since birth, was a cleaning maid.

There was also a gardener. The gardener's name was Fu-han, and he was Dongmei's second son.

Grandmother's work was very hard. She scrubbed tiled floors, swept the courtyard two times a day, and carried coal briquettes to the little stoves inside the house. She shared a small room with the maid who could not speak. They learned to talk to each other with hand signs.

All was peaceful in the household for many months. Beautiful Wife and Rich Landowner were often away in another city on business. Dongmei was very kind to my grandmother once she learned that her family back in the village were killed by the foreign devils. Dongmei knew about having a family member killed. Her husband had died when he was a guard for the landowner. There had been an attack by bandits while on a journey to an outer province. They'd gone to see the family land holdings. You know, land they owned where peasants worked for them. The peasants gave the landowner part of the money from the sale of their crops and animals every year. That's why the landowner was so rich and powerful and needed a body guard. Sometimes the peasants got angry and became bandits. They could not survive because the landowner took so much from them. Let me go back to the real story.

It must have been a terrible attack. Dongmei's husband saved the landowner's life, but only after he was wounded fighting off the peasants who had become bandits. He died two days later from his wounds. His heroic actions meant that Dongmei and her second son Fu-han would have their places with the rich family until they both died. That's how the grateful landowner honored the man who had saved his life. I forgot to tell you that her second son was a very strong young man with a weak mind. He could do the work as the gardener quite well, but about other things he was what they called simple-minded. Sure, Carol, it meant mental disability like we say today when a kid can only learn so much and will never get any farther than about third grade. The children in the streets were cruel to him. Whenever they saw Fu-han as he trimmed the trees around the big house or cleaned the koi pond outside the gate, they would yell at him and call him Frog. They jumped around like frogs and made sounds like croaking frogs, but Fu-han never paid attention to their taunts. No, these weren't the children of the rich people. The bullies were children who begged outside the gates and were chased away each day by the servants of the big houses. Koi? That's a Chinese fish. You know, the big fat bright golden ones. Hey, let's stay with the story.

Everything went very well for Chun Tao in her new job until one day Beautiful Wife made an announcement to all the servants. Her husband's nephew had returned from studies abroad. Yeah, maybe it was London or someplace like that. He must have been able to speak English as well as Chinese, huh? The nephew would live at his uncle's house while he started his own business in the city. He planned to be a moneylender. I think that is what Grandmother said. Anyway, some trade where he could make even more money than his uncle. Yes, they were all very rich from being born into very wealthy families. Yeah, like today—if you got it, you got it.

The nephew came to live with the family and right away things changed for the servants. The nephew brought home many of his companions who demanded service of food and drinks at different hours than the usual times. Rich Landowner was away most of the time and didn't know about lavish meals and bottles of rice wine the friends consumed. Money from the household account was being spent twice as fast as usual, but somehow Beautiful Wife made up reasons why the money needed to be replenished each month in greater amounts. The servants served extravagant dinners to Beautiful Wife, the nephew, and his friends. These actions were a great scandal because married women were not allowed to talk freely with men other than their husbands. When Beautiful Wife smiled at the nephew, she thought the servants did not notice. My grandmother often saw the two of them as they left the compound out the back gate. They didn't come back for many hours. When the nephew and Beautiful Wife returned, they often wore a new expensive garment or new jewelry. Grandmother told me that they had bought each other gifts with her husband's money that was meant for the household. Of course, the servants didn't tell Old Landowner about the terrible behavior of Beautiful Wife, but the servants were worried. I guess they were afraid of what the Old Landowner might do if he found out his wife had brought dishonor upon him.

You know, dishonor. She was messing around with the nephew. Duh! Oops, sorry about the "duh" again. Guess she thought her husband loved her so much and thought she was so beautiful that she could get away with it. But guess what? Bet you can figure it out. Beautiful Wife realized her husband was suspicious about how much money she had spent. Dongmei had informed Beautiful Wife that supplies were disappearing at an alarming rate because of the many parties the nephew gave. More money was needed to run the household. Beautiful Wife's nephew proposed a plan that would repay the money into the account so his uncle would not know about the missing funds. If the money was returned to the household account, Beautiful Wife could cover up her dishonorable actions. Yeah, they were big into honor and dishonor and how it was going in that department.

At the end of the year many holidays were celebrated. The Landowner wanted to take his wife to visit his mother's family. They would be away for seven days. The nephew said he and his friends would journey to see The Great Wall. He lied to the uncle about his situation, of course. He wanted to stay behind in the city with his friends. He and Beautiful Wife had a plan. What? Oh good, you guessed. Yes, they had a thing, you know, lovers. He promised to return the money that had been overspent in the household accounts she handled. She made him promise to do this so her husband would no longer be suspicious of her. Oh, you think this story reminds you of a very long movie you watched with your mom one time? She took you to the cinema across town? I know, the one you have to take the bus to get there. Well, this story does have an adult theme, but you're getting old enough to know about these things. Adults do mess up their lives. When you find out how they messed up it's supposed to be a warning not to do the same. So where was Grandmother in all this? I guess you want to know what happens about Frog, too. You got it. The story doesn't have a real frog, but the guy named Frog. Smart girl. Hey, enough. Let me finish.

The only ones left behind at the compound were Dongmei, her son Fu-han and Grandmother. None of them had any family to visit for the holidays. Grandmother had a few relatives who still lived outside the city, but no one wanted to be reminded of the terrible thing that had happened in the village. Peasants in the countryside were superstitious and thought Grandmother was bad luck.

They later learned of the nephew's plan to steal Beautiful Wife's jewels from the house. He would sell them to his drinking companions at a low price and have enough money to cover the account Beautiful Wife had overdrawn. Yeah, kind of lame, huh. But it's the story! And, of course, he was the beloved nephew and thought his uncle wouldn't suspect him. However, his uncle was a suspicious and jealous man.

The Landowner overheard some of the servants talking about his wife and his nephew. The night before the couple left for the holiday, he went to Dongmei and Frog in their rooms at the house. He also asked for Chun Tao, my grandmother to be present. They were told to watch carefully over the next week to see that no one entered the house. If anyone entered the house, Grandmother was to go to the authorities immediately, whether it was day or night. Grandmother told him that she did not know the proper streets that led to the places of authority. Fu-han spoke up that he would go with her to help find the way. Dongmei laughed when she heard her second son offer his help but when she saw the determined expression on her son's face, she did not speak up to change his mind. She hoped that her son did know the way, but she knew that Chun Tao would have to be the one to speak to the authorities. Fu-han was called Frog and no one would listen to a frog.

Yes, you have maybe already guessed what happened. On the second night after the landowner and his wife left on their journey, Dongmei, Fu-Han, and Grandmother were asleep with only two lanterns left burning in the dark shadowy courtyard. Grandmother first heard the sound of the wooden gate as it creaked open. She quietly woke up Dongmei and Fu-Han. They hid in empty cupboards that were next to Beautiful Wife's rooms.

They listened as footsteps echoed down the long hallway and then stopped in front of her door. They heard the sound of the large key as it turned to open the lock. Well, sure, the nephew had the key that had been given to him by Beautiful Wife. I know, it does get a little much with all the lover stuff, right? But this is the way Grandmother told me. They heard the person who entered the rooms make noises when pulling out the drawers in the chests where the jewelry was kept. Dongmei knew about the drawers with the expensive jewelry so that's how she knew what was being opened. The drawers were locked, but the thief opened them with another key given to him by his...you know, Beautiful Wife. The sound of a drawer being dropped on the floor surprised the three who hid in the cupboards. Fu-han gave a huge gasp that could have been heard by the person in the room. A stream of angry words echoed in the room and then silence. In the silence that followed, the three servants kept very still until they heard the door close and the key turn in the lock. Heavy footsteps ran down the hall.

They ran from their hiding place, rushed to the

upper windows to look into the courtyard and saw the nephew who stepped out of the front door. He stood for a moment under the two lanterns and then began to run. A red sash from his clothing flew loose as he ran out of sight. The nephew wasn't very smart, was he? He left the dropped drawer and then locked the door. Anyone who reads mystery stories knows that was a mistake. I know you like mystery stories but usually they are about kids who solve the problems, not Chinese lovers, correct? I'm getting off track from the story, aren't I?

So...the cops would know it was someone who had a key, right? Well, guess it would not be cops in this story, but "the official authorities." And, oh yeah, Dongmei picked up the red sash the nephew left behind and gave it to Grandmother and her second son to show what the thief had left behind. Everyone in the household knew that the nephew wore expensive red sashes. In fact he had many red sashes of different designs that had been gifts from Beautiful Wife. The red sash was evidence against the nephew who was supposed to be out of the city.

The nephew had been pretty wrong about his friends. One of his friends to whom he tried to sell the jewels informed on him to the authorities. To make this long story shorter, by the time old

Landowner and cheating Beautiful Wife had returned from the holiday, the nephew had been locked up in the cell where they put thieves waiting for sentences from the judge. The authorities wanted to question Beautiful Wife since the nephew had confessed that she knew what he had planned to do. You can't imagine how enraged the Landowner was when he found out that Beautiful Wife had planned the robbery because the two were lovers. He had been dishonored.

The Landowner sent Beautiful Wife away the very next day. No, no one knew where she was sent, but it was forever. The Landowner rewarded Dongmei, Fu-han, and my grandmother for their obedience and courage. Each were given a bag of coins which was six month's extra wages. Grandmother said that for the rest of the time she worked at the house, the other servants laughed and mockingly called their good fortune "Frog's Reward" as if they could not believe the loyalty of a simple boy, his mother, and the lowly maid. Actually, the other servants were very jealous, don't you think? Grandmother always gave credit to Frog, I mean Fu-han, for running with her to the place of the authorities. He was the one who handed the red sash to the head officer and gave the nephew's name. It took a lot of courage since many people did not usually believe what a simple boy says.

**

"Yeah, that's it. The story about a frog. Maybe not the kind you thought it would be, but still a frog story, except with a capital "F" since it was a name for the simple boy."

Carol did not speak at first, but then took a deep breath. "Your stories are kinda weird. Are you trying to teach me something with these stories?"

"Why do you say that?"

"I dunno."

"Hmmm...don't be that way. I like telling stories and you like listening. Telling and listening equals learning." Charity spoke with a stern voice.

"Yeah, but I want to know about things, too. Like why do you only tell stories that are about your grandmother? And why do you shuffle those cards all the time?"

"They help me remember the stories."

"Oh. Now that's the kind of thing I like to know. Why people do stuff and what it means."

"That's what I think about a lot, too. Guess we are in tune with each other." Charity gave Carol a lopsided smile.

"In tune? You mean understanding each other? I

don't know much about you because you have never told me anything about yourself. Where do you live? Who are your parents? What school do you go to?"

"Hey, let's just stay in tune with each other and go from there. Anyway, I think you are going to be late getting home today. The days are getting shorter now. Better get back home." Charity was calm and nonchalant.

"Sure. You don't want to tell me anything. I get it. See you around." Carol's face burned with indignation, but she was immediately sorry she'd lost her temper with her new friend.

"Well, I'll be around again." Charity put the cards in the side pocket of her sleek black jacket. She adjusted her black hat with the purple trim. "I hope you will come tomorrow."

Carol walked home slowly. She never once turned to see if Charity still sat on the bench or if she had left. Her thoughts were about the stories and what each one meant. A protective unicorn and a dead family, a flood and a treasure, a journey that didn't end well, Chinese lovers and a boy named Frog. Four days, four different stories that had a lesson for her. If only she could figure it all out. She vowed to do drawings of each story and that would help her understand. She hoped Charity's word was good and that they would meet again.

25

DAY FIVE—FRIDAY

ALICE

Alice awoke and glanced at the clock by her bed—already a few minutes after six and Friday, last day of classes for the week. Alice had not turned off her computer until just before midnight Thursday night when she completed her attempts to rework two papers due for her Friday ten o'clock class. She knew she hadn't put in her best effort on them. She might get a B grade, but maybe not even that. Graduate students couldn't make anything lower than a B. She felt certain the papers would be returned for revision. She would only have one more chance to maintain her B average or be asked to drop the classes. Failure's not an option for grad students. One can say they quit grad school, but never that one failed. After staying up so late at her computer agonizing over the final drafts, she stayed awake for another hour sitting in the darkened bedroom. She had gone over in her mind the stories she heard in the last four days. Each story should have a lesson for her, what the underlying meanings might be. A family killed in a village, a flood that killed valuable cows, a journey that ended—well, she did not really know the ending, only that it seemed to be a journey that did not end well—and then a story about a jewel theft and a simple minded man called Frog. The very strange stories unsettled her. She usually could interpret events and relationships, but these stories and their meanings haunted her every thought.

Today she would question Angel. That is, if Angel made an appearance again. She hoped Angel would help her make sense of her experience at the fountain since she couldn't shake the feeling she had a vision; she did not understand why she woke up in Angel's presence. Also, the pagoda puzzled her—the beautiful pagoda looked different every day. What did it symbolize for her? Just looking at it made her feel safe. Then it came to her why she felt that way. It reminded her of her blissful childhood before she was on her own and in a troubled relationship with her mother. College friends always teased her that she tried to find meaning in every little thing she saw. Alice, however, hoped life had real meaning and she often wondered what lessons she could learn from every day encounters. Maybe the pagoda symbolizes my former life and the fountain points to my future. The faceless cherub looked up because I can't see my future.

Alice didn't run this morning. Tired from lack of sleep, she purposely walked a steady pace into the park, determined to sort out all her thoughts about the stories and find meaning in them. When she saw the path ahead, she felt a sense of purpose as she stepped onto the gravel that crunched beneath her shoes. On the bench ahead, she saw a figure in the bright sunlight. The person held an open umbrella above her head even though the sky had no rain clouds. *Yes, it's Angel!* As Alice neared the bench, Angel dropped the open umbrella onto the ground and smiled sweetly at her.

"It's not raining, Angel. Why were you holding the umbrella over your head?"

Angel's look of infinite patience told Alice there wouldn't be an answer to the question.

"Well, hello to you, too, young lady. Why aren't you doing your exercise today?"

"The same reason you were holding an open umbrella over your head when it's not raining. No reason, I suppose. Just changed up my routine."

"Such impertinence, my dear, in your answer to my question. If you must know, I get inspiration from my umbrella. Is that enough of an answer for you?" Angel was firm.

"You've been here for five days in a row." Alice ventured the comment to change the subject.

"Yes. Do you mean that as a question or a statement?"

"Well, I have a reason to come every day. It's my routine...time I need for myself."

"Unlike you, my routine, as you call it, isn't for myself," sighed Angel.

"Oh, then just for me? Or do you have other people who stop and listen to your stories? You always come at the same time, just as I do."

"You hold dear your routines and your ideas, young woman. It is usually old women like me who do that."

Alice realized that Angel had not answered her question about telling stories to other people in the park. She rephrased her question.

"How long do you stay each day after telling me a story? Do you repeat the same story to the others who come by?"

"What others?" Angel's expression was a look of amusement.

"Other people you tell your stories to. That is your purpose here, isn't it?"

"Everyone has a purpose and stories have a meaning. I know you wish for purpose and meaning. Shall I start another story or have you heard enough?"

Alice paused before answering. Angel seemed to have insights into Alice's thoughts. *I won't ask about the fountain after all. It meant I lost my way, but I can recover. I'm learning the lessons.*

"Of course I haven't heard enough. I want to hear more and understand what it is all about."

"It? You mean your life?"

Alice murmured her reply. "Yes, my life."

Angel smiled at Alice with a patient look once again.

26

DAY FIVE—THE STORY OF A CIRCUS ANGEL

I had never been to a circus until I was older and lived in the city. I did not know what happened when people went to the big tent erected on outskirts of town. My friends spoke of the circus with excitement when the posters began to appear. They told me that a circus included a fine band of musicians, jugglers, painted clowns, prancing horses, dancing bears, little dogs that jumped through hoops, beautiful women in spangled costumes, and muscular male weight lifters. After leaving my position at the large house, I found other suitable employment. I sold flowers, a delightful and satisfying occupation. I had a small booth in the largest flower market in the whole country. Please, don't ask me again what country, my dear. You don't need that information to enjoy the story.

During the flower season I sold fresh flowers, and during the cooler months I sold large beautiful dried wreaths that were bought for holiday decorations. I learned to craft the wreaths from an old woman who wove baskets. Her basket table stood close to my flower stand at the market. Her hands had stiffened with age so it took her a very long time to make baskets. I paid her a little from each wreath I sold as payment for her instructions. Everyone said I had a natural gift for weaving baskets and fashioning them to look like the flowers I had arranged when I worked for Madame at the large house. The flowers spoke to me and I to them. You have never heard of flowers speaking? Not in the literal sense, but symbolically, of course, my dear. Do you always live in a literal world? Learn to use your imagination. That's what I tell those who see the world in a narrow way. Yes, I am telling you this because you need a lesson in imagination. Now, shall I continue about the circus?

Of course, a circus is all imagination and illusion. Children who grew up in the villages did not know of such things as circuses. We had heard of bands of travelers who were traders and entertainers, but my village was so small they bypassed us. I am sure you cannot imagine living in such a small place. The forlorn village where I lived did not compare to the nice town where you grew up. How did I know you grew up in a nice town, not this place? Why, I guess you could call it my imagination, my dear. I could not imagine that you had always lived in this very large city where you find yourself now. I can tell by the way you appreciate the beauty of the park. City people don't take time to do such things, do they? Back to my storytelling, please.

The circus advertisements stated that the performances would be presented every evening for ten days. One small coin gained entrance for each night. I decided I would attend the circus every evening the performances were held. Ten days of performances seemed a good bargain for ten small coins. I was intrigued why the performers had chosen the life of the circus. One of my strongest traits had always been my curiosity about people. My dear, must you interrupt again? Yes, yes, my curiosity about people does help my storytelling. Your interruptions do not help the storytelling. Thank you for the apology. I will continue.

After one evening, I fell in love with the beautiful concept of the circus and also with a handsome man.

Boris trained the prancing white horses, one of the main acts of the circus. His act, the last of the evening, came right after the dancing bears, handled by a cruel man who seemed to delight in wielding a large prod to force the bears to dance and balance on small boxes. Boris was different. His gentleness and expertise with the beautiful horses enthralled the audience. When he rode two of them at a time standing on their bare backs with leather reins in his hand, my heart beat faster and faster until I felt faint. I was transfixed by his shining pale blond hair and his muscular body.

For the climax of his performance he invited someone in the crowd into the ring while the six horses stood in a circle. At his command, the lovely horses, one by one, bowed to the center with their snow white manes laced with multi-colored ribbons and small bells falling almost to the ground. Boris would whisper something into the ear of the person. Once or twice the chosen one would stand for several seconds unable to respond. Boris would gently touch the person to break their spell of amazement. Once the person raised both hands and clapped three times as Boris had instructed in the whisper, the horses stood up, shook their manes and stamped the ground as the crowd applauded. It was a beautiful scene.

On the third night I sat as close to the ring as I could. I had taken great care to choose my most flattering dress and hat. Purple, of course, my favorite color as you have observed. You have guessed what happened I am sure. Boris chose me from the audience that night. He whispered into my ear the command to make the horses stand up. I stood still for the second prompt by Boris. I had understood the first time but I wanted him to whisper in my ear twice. The second time he whispered that he would wait outside the tent close to the horses' corral after the show. He asked me to meet him. You can imagine my complete happiness.

I met Boris after the performances for the next seven nights. Each night we fell more in love. He implored me to join him when the circus left the city. We would be together—yes, a thrilling life on the road where I would help him with the beautiful horses, traveling to faraway and exotic places. Boris promised to teach me to tell fantastic stories about the horses that would captivate the audiences and add more drama to the performances.

No, he wasn't my first love. My first love left me to join the army and serve the motherland. There was another complication at this time. You see, I had already promised myself to a middle-aged butcher at the market. My great-aunt Hilda, my only living relative, urged me to marry and be settled. I agreed that marriage to an established and successful butcher would be a wise choice. I had convinced myself that I would come to love the butcher. He was a kind man whose wife died giving birth to their first child. The child died three days later. That happened quite frequently in those days. He had been a widower for ten years. In his youth I am sure he would have been considered handsome. In middle age he had lost most of his hair and was rather stout. He needed a wife so he would not be lonely in his old age. Other homely girls like me who worked in the market tried to catch his eye, but he settled his interest on me from the first day I set up my flower stand. This is called a dilemma, correct? I had a decision to make, a life-changing decision.

Now tell me, how should this story end, my young friend? What ending would you choose? A life of settled contentment and security? A life of constant travel and adventure? Now think carefully, my dear, because one never knows ahead of time, which choice will really be for the best, do we? You say you hope I went with my heart? But there's the logical mind one must deal with, too. You must decide the ending.

**

"Alice, that's the end of my stories. You must decide your story now. Time for you to go on with your morning routine. I think you will be later than usual getting back."

Alice did not try to conceal her disappointment with the way Angel dismissed her. She felt deflated as if she had been pumped up for a big surprise at the end of the story and it fell through. Yet, she understood the lesson about choices.

"Why are you telling me stories, Angel? I've been here for five mornings in a row. This is the second time you have told me to make up the ending of your story. Each day your stories become more elusive, more difficult to understand the point."

"Do stories have a point or a lesson for you? I want my stories to have lessons for the recipient."

"But stories should have a point. You know, the point is what the story is trying to get across to the person hearing it. And a story should make me feel emotion. Stories should make me happy or sad, but your stories leave me confused." Alice looked bewildered as she spoke.

"You care only about being happy or sad? There are many other emotions, young lady. Confusion is an emotion. Maybe it is one you should appreciate as much as happiness. You should think about points and lessons. I don't agree with the concept of making a point, or whatever one does with a point. It's a most unsatisfactory word to use about stories."

Alice did not reply but looked at her watch. Unless she left soon she would not be at her ten o'clock class to turn in the papers. The professor wouldn't understand if she was late because she listened to an eccentric old woman telling stories in the park. *What is the point? That word again. Or should it be a lesson for me? The lesson learned for late papers was an incomplete grade.* She didn't want to share these thoughts with Angel.

"I'm going to be late if I don't leave now, but I want to talk more with you."

"Tardiness becomes a habit difficult to break." Angel's comment startled Alice.

"I have a choice, don't I, Angel?"

"Yes, my dear, you do. Perhaps you should think about it before we discuss the matter. You must be on your way."

"I'll come tomorrow. It's Saturday. My usual time...seven o'clock?"

"My schedule changes for the Sabbath. Perhaps later in the morning. Ten would be best."

"Thank you, Angel, for today. I do need a lesson. I need to make a choice. OK, I'll be here tomorrow at ten instead of seven."

Alice didn't jog or walk briskly back to the apartment. She knew she wouldn't make the deadline. She walked slowly and observed the bare sycamore trees and the tall grayish green spruces, the low walls beside the gravel path, the leafless branches of rose bushes with dried blossoms. She listened to the sounds of unseen twittering birds, the long sad horn of a tugboat on the river and sharp cries of large gulls that circled the river banks. As the wind rustled dry leaves on the path, her attention was riveted on the harsh chatter of two squirrels that chased each other up a large tree. She breathed deeply the musty smell of decayed vegetation, the dry baked smell of the stone walls exposed to the morning sun, and strong whiff of the slightly metallic smell of river water. She felt the warm morning sun on her shoulders when a slight breeze ruffled her hair. She felt at one with the park and everything in it, all the sights and sounds of nature she loved. She felt alive.

27

DAY FIVE—FRIDAY

BEA

Bea awoke with a terrible headache. She couldn't shut the alarm off fast enough. *Why did I buy the one with such an annoying buzzer? Surely there are some pleasant sounds to wake me up. Probably cost a lot more than two dollars from the Goodwill bin. I did get a bargain.*

"My head. My head," she said aloud and Sweetie perked up his ears like he hoped Bea would take him into the small backyard for his morning business. But instead, Bea stumbled to the small bathroom and rummaged through the bottles on the shelf. *No more aspirin. First thing in the morning a headache and no aspirin. What a day.* Almost every day Bea thought to herself, "What a day." She sometimes said it out loud in an aggrieved tone to show her displeasure with whatever she felt not right at the moment. It might be that the neighbor left a pile of empty boxes by the front steps of the building, or the trashcan had been tipped over by a roaming cat during the night, or perhaps her morning newspaper had been dropped too close to the stairway. "We won't go out today, Sweetie," she said firmly. "I don't feel well."

A little later as she sat eating her morning bowl of Rice Krispies she felt better and changed her mind. Once again she addressed Sweetie, "We will go out. I feel better. But today I'm going to talk to that Bounty. I'm gonna find out a few things that are bothering me." Sweetie looked at Bea as if he understood English. Poor Sweetie, it was English spoken as a complaint because that was the tone Bea used when she spoke. Bea fumed over Bounty's continued cheerfulness and how she seemed to take pleasure in telling such unbelievable stories about her own mother's life. *Too many unusual experiences for one person. Unbelievable. What kind of gullible person did the woman think I am? Believing those stories, humph!* She recounted to herself the tales she had heard in the last four days. *First, the utterly strange one about a unicorn that saved Bounty's mamá's life. No such animal as a unicorn! The second day she told about a flood that killed a bunch of dumb chickens and washed up a bag of priceless little dolls. Who could possibly think that would happen? A story about a journey and her mama left singing on a doorstep was one Bounty did not even finish telling. And then just yesterday a fourth story about some lovers who stole jewels and a boy named Frog. Bounty made me finish up the story myself!* Yet she felt she had somehow been captured by the stories and they had troubled her. Usually she didn't acknowledge feelings she had other than annoyance or disgust, but she felt different in the last few days. Different, in that she thought about how she always was dissatisfied with her life. *What would it be like to be cheerful and pleasant like Bounty who sat on a park bench and told stories?*

At the usual time, Bea led Sweetie out the door and walked at a slightly slower pace than usual. She wanted to think of questions she would ask Bounty. As she approached the now familiar gravel path, she felt a sense of purpose for her time in the park. Sweetie walked beside her and didn't pull but trotted happily. As she looked toward the bench she saw Bounty, dressed as usual, standing by the bench surrounded by pigeons and tossing crumbs in semi-circles on the path in front of her. One small white pigeon perched on the arm of the bench. The pagoda shone in the noontime sun.

"There are more birds than usual," said Bea, an abrupt first comment to Bounty.

"It is a lovely thing that they come for a free meal."

"They are freeloaders, for sure."

"Why do you always think opposite of happy?"

"Opposite of happy?"

"You know what I mean, Bea. You see the bad things, not the happy, so you think opposite of happy."

"I had never heard it put that way before. My co-workers always called me grumpy."

"Grumpy the same as bad temper?"

"Yes, I suppose so but I would rather be called grumpy than bad tempered. Probably the same to some people, though."

"You have not gone to look inside the pagoda yet. Want to do that today?"

"Why would I want to do that today?'

"Maybe it would make you happy, not grumpy. Go on, I will feed my birds and wait here for you."

Bea was usually stubborn when someone made a

suggestion that wasn't her idea, but something came over her. She thought it would be a good idea to take Bounty's suggestion. She was somewhat curious about the little building.

"Here, you hold Sweetie's leash. Down, Sweetie. Stay. He'll be OK and I'll go take a quick look."

"We'll be right here on the bench waiting for you, little Sweetie dog and me."

Bea reluctantly walked toward the pagoda. She wondered why Bounty insisted that today she look at the pagoda. Bounty put a meaning on everything and had acted as if this was very important for her to inspect the strange building. The structure looked shabby with paint that peeled off the outside walls. The metal roof looked dented and slightly rusted. Spider webs hung from the corners of the building. Dead leaves had piled against the walls. Bea thought the city should have torn it down years ago. *It was probably a hazard, containing some of that asbestos.* Bea would take a quick look to satisfy Bounty's insistent request. She hadn't noticed anything unusual on the day Sweetie ran in and she'd dragged him out.

When she stepped through the teardrop shaped entrance out of the glaring noonday sun, it took her eyes a moment to adjust. She expected some type of furniture inside or walls lined with benches for seating, but there were no benches, nothing on the dusty floor but more dead leaves that had blown in. She stood for a moment feeling rather disappointed that Bounty made so much of her looking at the pagoda as if there was really something to see. She took one more look around the inside before she turned to leave. A small tapping sound coming from the ceiling made her look up. What she saw was one of the biggest surprises she'd had in a long time. The ceiling was painted with several shades of blue, from very pale to blindly bright hues, a kaleidoscope of blues. The colors swirled and blended together in patterns she had never seen. Blue was Bea's favorite color, and this display made her feel happy. Happy wasn't a feeling she experienced on a regular basis. The shades of blue momentarily soothed her bad-tempered attitude. She felt at peace with herself. She wondered if Bounty had known this would happen. Bea lingered for a few more moments and then walked out of the pagoda into the sunlight. Bounty and Sweetie waited patiently for her at the bench.

"That was a big surprise!"

"You liked it, yes?"

"Who could have painted a ceiling in such a way? Blue is my favorite color."

"*Si*, I know."

"We never talked about colors," said Bea.

Bounty ignored the remark. "The pagoda is really very old and has good history."

"History? Looks like it should be torn down, except they could save the blue ceiling. Maybe it could be preserved by the city. The city tears down some old things and preserves others all the time."

"You don't have much respect for the city that paid you all those years."

"Well, the city is a hard place...how did you know I worked for the city? Another thing we never talked about. How do you know these things about me?"

"Well, I think about people I meet. Things come to me."

"Come to you? Are you saying you read minds?" Bea sounded very skeptical.

"No, that's not what I am saying to you. We are forgetting why we are here. Ready for another story?"

"Hmm...why we are here, you say. I have been wondering why you are always here at the bench. I have a routine to walk my dog every day. Why are you here? The birds don't need your crumbs to live. Telling stories to strangers seems like an odd routine." These were questions Bea wanted answered.

"Everyone needs a routine. Everyone certainly needs stories. We really must start the story for today."

"I've been here for the last four days and listened to your stories. I'll sit again today if you tell me one that makes sense. The stories are always about your mamá. Why is that?"

"Why not stories about my mamá? She was a good person and learned many lessons in her life. She taught me many lessons, too. Maybe you need lessons, Bea."

Bea just nodded. Bounty started a new story.

28

DAY FIVE—THE STORY OF A CIRCUS BOUNTY

Once my mamá went to a circus. Maybe it wasn't really a circus as we say today, but it was a traveling show that entertained people in villages and poor parts of cities. There were clowns, magicians, music, and wonderful stories told to the crowds. The shows did not cost much since poor people could not afford to pay very much. It was a special day when adults went to the circus. Most of the children sneaked into the shows. The performers understood and did not chase them away. I think there were many young ones who wanted to run away and join the circus. My mamá's great uncle said he was once a singing clown, but no one believed him because most of the singing clowns were black, not *mestizo* like him. *Si,* Bea, black the same as you. My mamá, Blanca, saved to buy a ticket since the first day she saw posters that announced when the show would arrive. Several of the women from the bakery where she worked asked if she would join them to see the circus. I remember her telling me how very excited she was to be invited. She had very few friends in the city. She had been lonely since Cousin Maria had left for a position as a French teacher at a small school in the capital city far away.

The first night she went to the performance she fell in love. *Si,* it was a man, not a handsome man like a romance story, but a man with a beautiful voice who told wonderful stories. He was short, dark-skinned, dark black wavy hair, and light green eyes that sparkled when he told the stories. The voice he possessed was *muy grande.* His voice made all the girls fall in love with him when they heard his stories. My mamá was no different from the others who saw him perform that first night. The next morning as she and her friends baked breads and cakes, they talked about the man with the story-telling voice. Mamá decided that she would meet him before the circus left town.

The next evening my mamá went by herself to the

tent at the edge of the city. Although she did not have enough money to buy a ticket, she thought of a way she might be able to enter. Always at the end of the day, the owner gave his workers some of the leftover bread or pastries. The bakery owner did not pay them very well, but he did not want any of them to go hungry. It was his way of keeping his workers happy enough to return to work the next day.

Mamá decided the try to sell three bread loaves and a small bag of little cakes she had received. That way she would have enough to buy a ticket. As she stood at the entrance to the big tent, she held the loaves in her hands and a strange thing began to happen. The stale breads sent out a delicious warm baked smell. The smell tickled the noses of those who had lined up to buy tickets. Two small boys standing in line with their papá immediately noticed the pleasant smell of bread. The boys begged their papá to buy a loaf from her. He paid my mamá a few pesos for the bread. When two women nearby saw the children eating the good-smelling bread, they wanted some for themselves. In only a few minutes, Mamá had enough money to buy a ticket.

A miracle! That's what she called what happened because it meant that she met the man with the beautiful voice that very night. You do not believe in miracles, Bea? Remember it is a story, too, so stories can have miracles, no? I think stories are miracles, but I can tell you don't. What happened that night changed my mamá's life for good. Do I mean for good or for the good? I do not get your meaning. You can hear and then you decide if it was for good or for the good for Blanca, my mamá. Such a fuss you are making over one little word.

The man with the voice like a melody heard about my mamá selling bread to buy a ticket. One of the clowns had told him about her beauty, too. Before his story telling started, he found Mamá seated in the last row at the back of the tent. He said to her, "Hello, my name is Jose. May I ask you to help me with my story tonight? I would be honored to be assisted by such a beautiful girl." Jose was a charmer, yes he was. He always asked someone from the crowd to help, but usually he choose an older child who could read. He assumed my mamá could read. When he told his stories, the person would hold up different colored signs that would help with the storytelling. Oh, you have not seen that type of story before? The helper would hold up a sign that told the crowd to do certain things like clap, whistle, boo and hiss, or even sing a few bars of a popular song. It was all a part of his storytelling and made the story funny or even sad at times. I am sure my mamá looked very beautiful that night dressed all in white with a purple flower in her hair. She told me that's what she wore the second night of the circus. Sure, my mamá liked to dress in white like I do. Her name was Blanca. Her name means white and she dressed in white. What do you mean about a clue? I am not sure I get your meaning about a clue, such a strange English word. I will keep telling, OK?

Well, the storyteller showed my mamá the large cards she was to hold up when he nodded in her direction. She was to hold up the card for each part of the story. My mamá was afraid to tell him that she did not read. No, no, she learned later to read when she found out how important it was for her life. Once the storytelling started all the crowd listened with great attention to Jose, the great storyteller. When he nodded at Mamá, she held up one of the cards that she hoped was the right word. The crowd laughed and laughed. Jose kept telling the story. Every time he nodded and she held up a card, the same thing happened. The crowd enjoyed the story and kept laughing. At the end of the story when Jose bowed with a great flourish, the crowd clapped for a long time. Jose came to Mamá and gave her kiss on each check as he pulled her to the front of the stage. He presented her to the crowd who clapped for another long time. Jose was very pleased with what had happened. People liked his story very much and what Mamá did entertained them even more.

Of course, when he told her that she had held up the wrong cards at the wrong time, Mamá broke into tears. She was very ashamed because she could not read. Jose took her in his arms and wiped her tears telling her that together they could make many people enjoy the stories. And that's how my mamá joined the circus and traveled to many provinces far from her home. So you see, Bea, sometimes you never know what one night at a circus will bring into your life. You want to know if they married? Hmmm, well, Mamá never told me she married Jose but she traveled with the circus for many years. Jose took very good care of her. Jose became famous on the radio after he left the circus. Many of the people in that country who became well-known on the radio started by telling stories or singing in the circus. The people in the villages and cities who had seen the circuses and knew the names of the singers and storytellers. All the villagers faithfully listened to radio stories. Many storytellers became very wealthy. No, my mamá did not become wealthy or famous because she married my papá who was not in the circus. That is another story. Mamá never told me where she met my papá and I never asked.

**

Bea was sorry to hear Bounty's story end the way it did. While she listened, she was sure that Blanca had married Jose. That was her idea of a proper ending to such a story.

"Why do your stories have strange endings?"

"The ending is the ending. I can't change the stories." Bounty said cheerfully.

"But people hearing stories expect endings that are satisfactory."

"Satisfactory? That means different things to different people, I think."

"Don't you want me to be satisfied with your stories?" Bea demanded.

"You are missing the meanings, I'm afraid. My stories teach lessons."

"I am too old for lessons. I know what life is and what to expect."

"You must think about that more. Can you ever know what life will bring?"

Bounty began to gather up the empty bread bags around her feet. The small white pigeon waddled from behind a line of bushes beside the path. She straightened her hat slightly and then looked at Bea as if to say "Now what?"

Bea wanted to make herself clear about what the next day would bring. "I come every day at the same time. Tomorrow is Saturday. Will you be here tomorrow again?"

"Saturday is the day I come in the morning. I am here by ten." Bounty nodded knowingly as she spoke.

"Sweetie and I will come then, too. It will be early for us. Maybe I will figure out the lesson you think I need."

"OK, we both come tomorrow. *Buenos dias.*"

Bea left the park with a feeling of satisfaction. She thought the tale of a storyteller in the circus much more believable than Bounty's other stories. *Well, maybe not the miracle bread.* It was clear to her that Bounty's fondness of storytelling came from her mother. *Was it a usual thing that families passed down stories?* Bea tried to think of some happy family stories she had learned from her childhood, but all she remembered were the hard times she'd had growing up with five siblings. No man was around the house to teach her two good-for-nothing brothers to be responsible men. She decided when she got back to the apartment she would look through old boxes of family photos. Maybe the photos would remind her of family members and happy stories she had heard. She hadn't thought about her family for a long, long time.

29

DAY FIVE—FRIDAY

CAROL

Carol sat in sixth period art class gazing out the window at a beech tree with yellow leaves. The tree was across the street from the school in front of an older brownstone that had a "For Lease" sign in front. The type of place her mom could not afford. There was a nice little wrought iron gate around the front steps and white starched curtains in the first floor windows. Carol daydreamed about living in such a large place. She'd have her own bedroom that she'd painted herself in her favorite color, blue. A white four poster bed with a white quilted bedspread and white fluffy pillows completed the picture in her head. Her daydreams spun on and on about a bedroom she would never have. Carol wanted to ask her mom about the difference in renting and leasing a place to live. She remembered overhearing her mom on the phone talking about the high cost of rent. Her daydreams were cut short by Miss Brandt tapping her on the shoulder.

"Carol, you didn't turn in your assignment for the week yet. You haven't been working in class today so I assume you completed the work. Did you do more pencil sketches or did you attempt the watercolors?

"I did the pencils. I need more practice to get the watercolors right."

"May I see what you did?"

Carol pulled from her folder two small drawings. They were the ones she had done of things she'd seen in the park. Miss Brandt looked very impressed with what she saw.

"Is this a real person or someone you imagined?" She looked at the one of a slender Asian girl with long braids sitting on an old-fashioned wrought iron park bench.

"She's real, but I did that one from memory."

"So this is someone you know?" Miss Brandt seemed very interested in the drawing.

"Sort of know her, I guess. I see her in the park. I wanted her to pose for me, but she couldn't that day.

We ran out of time."

"Well, it's excellent work. Do you think you captured her correctly from memory? That's often hard to do."

"I think so, but maybe I should take the drawing with me next time I see her to make sure."

"What about this one of the fountain with the three angels at the center?"

"Well, that one is hard to explain. I think I dreamed it but I'm not sure." Carol blushed as she tried to think of the right words about what had happened.

"Had you seen a fountain similar to it in the past?"

"No." Carol did not want to talk more about the fountain.

"Again, Carol, this is excellent work from you. I've told you that you are more advanced than the others. That's why I think private lessons would be good for you. You'll progress faster. Did you ask your mother about taking art classes at the studio?"

"No." Carol imagined a stone wall rising between her and Miss Brandt.

"I'll see that you don't have to pay the full fee. Will you ask your mother to contact me?"

"No, that's OK. I can't do it."

Miss Brandt continued to gaze at Carol's work for a few more minutes. Carol looked down at her hands on the desk. Miss Brandt's gaze was intense and she shook her head slowly as if to indicate she was sorry about Carol's answer. Carol did not want to take her suggestions about more art classes.

"All right, Carol. Your assignment for next week is to bring me another drawing of this girl and two more people. Practicing portraits is what I want you to do."

"Thanks, Miss Brandt. I'll try my best."

The bell rang ending the period. Carol quickly picked up her backpack and, for the first time ever, left the room without saying good-bye to Miss Brandt.

It usually took Carol a few minutes to walk to the park and turn off onto the path leading to the pagoda area. Today she slowed her steps and decided to sit on one of the plain steel benches in the main park before she walked to the beautiful iron bench. She concentrated on studying two people who passed. She tried to decide if she should use one of them for her new assignment. Both were in a hurry so she didn't get many details in her mind. Finally, she gave up. She knew that she wanted to be a little later today to meet Charity—that is, if she was even there today. Five days in a row might be too much to hope for. There were so many questions she wanted to ask the teenager. Maybe she should write some of them down so she wouldn't forget. She pulled a notebook from her backpack, found a blue pencil, and started to write. She wrote three questions.

1. Why do you act like you want to be my friend?
2. What do your stories mean?
3. Are you real?

Carol wanted Charity to answer the questions with no joking around. Those were serious questions and she would make her answer them. Carol wasn't sure how but that's what she intended.

When Carol arrived at the bench, Charity was standing over by the pagoda looking inside. The afternoon sun glinted off the silver slippers she wore.

"Hey!" Carol shouted even though she didn't mean to shout.

Charity turned around slowly.

"Hey, yourself. You're late today. How come?"

"I stopped to write down some stuff."

Charity crossed the path and came to the bench where Carol waited. She sat down and looked at Carol with anticipation.

"Well, how come you had to write something before you came?"

"Because I have some questions I want to ask you. I wrote them down so I wouldn't get mixed up and forget."

"Oh, you're interviewing me like a reporter or something?"

"Yeah, sure like a reporter. Don't make fun of me." Carol's feelings were hurt.

"Not making fun of you. Just curious about why you want to ask me questions."

Carol did not reply for a few seconds while she tried to gather her thoughts and remember the questions. She finally sneaked a peek at the paper where she wrote her questions.

"What I want to know most is, are you real?'

"What? You want to know if I'm real, as in a real person?"

"I drew your picture. My art teacher asked if you were a real person. I told her I saw you in the park, but I drew you from memory. I've thought about it and maybe you're not real."

"That's pretty funny, kid. Aren't we here talking to each other? Isn't this real?"

"Guess so." Carol paused. "Don't call me kid, remember."

"What's the next question? You did have more than one, correct?"

"What do your stories mean? Ick! I am getting the questions out of order."

"Well, maybe that will take a while to explain to you. Or maybe you should think about the stories and discover the meaning for yourself."

"I've been trying."

"Try harder, Carol, try harder," Charity said it with a very serious look that Carol had not seen before.

"Here goes another story if you are ready for it. This one is about a circus."

"Is your grandmother in this one again? I didn't know they had circuses in China. That's where your grandmother lived, right?"

"Of course, all countries have something like a circus. The circuses in China go back a couple of thousand years, can you believe it?"

"I think we get world history next year. A thousand years is a really long time to have had a circus."

"Yeah, the old emperors started them or something. Or maybe the poor people had them first. Maybe you should look that up when you have world history. So, do you want the story or not?"

Carol remembered Charity had answered only two questions. "Wait. I have another question."

"Give it to me."

"Why do you act like you want to be my friend?"

"I'm not acting."

"We are friends then? You are older than my other two friends."

"You have only two friends? That's pretty lame. Uh...I mean kinda sad, actually."

"Don't feel sorry for me. It's fine. Two friends is all I need."

Charity paused before she spoke again. "No, you forgot, Carol. You have three now."

"Start the story, please. I hope it's a good one today and not weird like the other ones."

30

DAY FIVE—THE STORY OF A CIRCUS CHARITY

When my grandmother learned *The Show of a Hundred Tricks* was coming to the town where she lived, she knew that it was something she must attend. Oh, meant to tell you, in China that's what they called a circus. It's hard to believe but those shows there were much older than, say, the ones in Europe in the Middle Ages. You have heard about that time, right? The ones in my grandmother's country began about two thousand years ago like I said before. Cool, huh? The emperors might have started them for their courts. Yeah, emperors were like kings. Lots of power and money for them. Lots of hard work for the poor people. You will have it all in world history next year. Hey, I am getting off the story already with so many explanations.

These circuses were big on acrobats, jugglers, people who spun plates and danced at the same time, puppets, music, stuff like that. People dressed up like animals and did really hard balancing acts. I guess they were short on captured animals. You're laughing! Grandmother told me there were trained bears in Chinese circuses, but that was a later time. You know, I did see something online about a bear eating a bicycling monkey during Chinese circus a couple of years ago. Gross, right? And it was right in front of everyone. Gross, gross. Well, my grandmother didn't see anything like that. She was at the old-fashioned circus, *The Show of a Hundred Tricks.*

Three or four years had passed since she worked as a maid. She had a much better job as the owner of a small noodle shop and employed one helper. She named the shop Chun Tao's Noodle Shop. Not too original using just her name like that, but she must have had success with the business. She rented a small house close to the shop, so I guess she made good money if she could afford a small house. Back to the circus, right?

The street kids passed out posters all over town saying world famous acrobats in the circus performed The Lion's Dance. Grandmother did not know what that meant until she saw the show. She told me it was a most beautiful dance and balancing act, the kind of act that would take many long, long hours of practice. The young man and woman who did the dance had trained since they were only four years old. She thought they were twins, but someone told her they were cousins who had been born on the same day at the same time. This was considered a good sign and meant they would be friends as well as cousins. I think you would have to be friends to be able to practice together as much as they did. The show would be in town for six nights. The poor people attended at night since everyone had to work during the day. Grandmother said the very rich city people paid for special shows in their private compounds while the poor people worked.

After seeing the show for the first time, Grandmother knew she wanted to be a part of the circus. She was a fast learner and had already done many things. She had been a pig farmer, a maid, and a noodle shop owner. She was known for her confidence. Yes, that's what it was—confidence, knowing she could learn anything and do it well if she was given a chance to prove herself. She taught me to have confidence, too. Back to the story.

Everyone who attended the shows applauded most loudly for the acrobats; however, Grandmother loved the singing acts the best. The singers were introduced by a crippled older man who would first tell the story of the song. Every song had a story. His storytelling before the songs made people laugh or cry. When people listened to the songs, they would laugh or cry again. She thought that a person who could make others laugh or cry by telling a story was the smartest person in the whole province. People did not notice how crippled the man was when they heard his stories. My grandmother wanted to meet the storyteller and ask to be his apprentice. She wanted to learn how to tell stories with the same power and emotion.

You can ask a question if you need to so badly. And don't hold up your hand! That looks like you're in class or something...it looks dumb. I don't know how he became crippled. I guess he sat in a chair on the stage. Good question. Your next one about apprentices is easy. Yeah, that was common to study under somebody famous. Apprentices learned skills like furniture making or forging bells, or doing artistic stuff like painting or writing. Sure, the famous artists took on apprentices to help them in their studios. You'd be a good apprentice, Carol. You're a quick learner.

So back to finish up with the story. Grandmother told me she was very bold when she asked Wen, the crippled man, if she could be his apprentice.

I knew you would want to know. His name meant "literate person." Yes, that means he could read and, of course, tell excellent stories that he had memorized.

The next night before the performance she stood in front of the tent and gave away some tasty small cakes she'd baked at her noodle shop. Each person got two small cakes, one to eat and one to use as she told them. Inside each cake she'd placed a piece of paper with her name written on it.

Yes, her cousin, the tutor for the child in the big house, had taught her to read and write in a basic way—what we call second grade. Most girls from the villages couldn't read or write at all. She asked the people who took the little cakes to throw one cake onto the stage after the first story Wen told and before the songs began. They were to shout, "A cake for your helpful apprentice." Other people in the crowd thought throwing the cakes was a part of the show planned in advance. Sure, Wen was very confused when cakes flew at him after he told the first story. He asked if someone from the crowd would come and remove the cakes and quick as anything Grandmother ran to the stage and gathered up the cakes. She broke open one and taking out the paper read aloud her name, Chun Tao. Everyone clapped and clapped and shouted her name over and over, "Cake for Chun Tao, cake for Chun Tao, the helpful apprentice." Deeply impressed with my grandmother's boldness and ability to entertain the crowd, he took her hand and announced to the crowd that she would be his helpful apprentice. She became like a daughter to Wen. They traveled many miles together with *The Show of a Hundred Tricks* while she learned to tell stories that would make people laugh and cry. I see you are smiling at the end of this story. I could have told the story in another way to make you cry, but you needed a happy ending today.

**

Carol smiled after Charity finished. "I loved the story today with a happy ending! Did it have a meaning, too?"

"What would you say is the meaning? Wasn't that

one of your questions?"

"Is a meaning the same as a lesson?"

"Well, not exactly, but could be close, I guess."

"To me the story meant that anyone can think of things to do to change their life. It must have been better to be an apprentice storyteller than working in a noodle shop."

"You might be getting the hang of things now."

"Oh, almost forgot. I want to do a sketch of you for class. Would you stay for just a little longer? I'll be fast." Carol started to rummage in her backpack for her pad and pencils.

"So you're sure I'm real now. OK, get started on a picture of me!"

Carol furiously drew bold lines across the paper. She had a look of total concentration. The outline of Charity's face appeared on the paper.

"Yep, you're real. Just turn your face toward me for a minute."

"I didn't say I would actually pose for you."

"Yeah, but you are, aren't you? Friends do things like that for each other, right."

"Right." Charity sat very still and gazed across the path at the pagoda. "This is good and will help you later," she said in a barely audible voice.

Carol stopped drawing and tilted her head to the

right. Her eyes were wide and full of questions.

"Of course, it'll help me later, Charity. I'll get an A in art!"

"OK, OK. That's enough of putting my face on paper."

"Hold still just another sec."

"You need to leave, Carol. Your mom will be worried. Does she know you've been coming to the park every day this week? Aren't you supposed to go straight home and wait for her to come home from work?"

"I'll tell her I'm learning lessons in the park and doing my art homework."

"And if she asks about what lessons, will you tell her about the stories?"

"Nope, that's just between us. She wouldn't understand. She's got lots of other stuff on her mind anyway. I may have to move away. I won't be close to the park."

Charity looked at Carol and did not speak.

"I'm going to be late getting home," Carol said as she quickly tucked the pad into the backpack.
"Do you come on Saturday? I could probably come when Mom goes to market."

"Well, if she goes to market around ten, that's when I often come on Saturday. Often, sometimes, usually. You get what I'm saying. I'm not promising. But it's sometimes at ten."

Carol picked up the backpack and said, "I might have to run home to make it in time. See you tomorrow!"

Carol never looked back as she ran down the path. She barely made it into the apartment and sat in the kitchen chair to catch her breath when she heard sounds at the front door.

"I'm home, honey."

Carol answered, "I'm here, Mom."

31

DAY FIVE—FRIDAY NIGHT

ALICE

Alice was exhausted. Friday, the end of a usual week, meant she had attended all of her two-hour grad classes, written two papers which had been turned in late, and volunteered four hours at the college library to fulfill an unpaid service requirement for her student loans. Two study groups on Wednesday and Thursday nights lasted from nine until past eleven. In addition, she had worked two afternoon shifts at the mall where she carefully set the water timers, fertilized a big clump of yellowed Chinese ivy, adjusted lights around several planters, trimmed dead ficus tree leaves. After several attempts over the last weeks to convince her supervisor that half of the lights should be removed from several displays, she didn't bother to bring up the subject. The plants had shriveled from excessive heat. Her only social life for the week was coffee two times with a new friend Stephanie, whom she had met at the student center.

Alice usually struck others as a stable person, but she'd felt unmoored all week. Her emotional energy had been spent on thoughts about her encounters with Angel. As she listened to the compelling stories, she pondered questions she'd never asked herself. *What will my life's story be ten years from now? Twenty? Thirty? When I'm Angel's age? And just how old is Angel? Have I learned lessons from my small reserve of life experiences? What am I meant to do?* She knew her time in grad school hadn't made her happy. She wanted her life to count for something bigger than planning where city streets should intersect. Her assignments for classes were poorly done, mostly from her own lack of interest. Yet, she expected that she could slog through three more semesters and receive a degree that might land her a job in a city planning department back in the Midwest. If she moved back home after graduation, maybe her mother would have broken up with Jeff by then. She and her mother might be able to rekindle a close relationship.

When Alice sat at the computer and scrolled through her emails to check in for assignments she knew immediately something was wrong when she saw the message from her advisor Tomas Martinez. She gasped when she read it.

"Please be advised that you are now on probation with the Graduate Institute for Urban Planning due to unsatisfactory and incomplete assignments. Your work is not up to the standards of our program. Please contact me no later than Monday noon to set an appointment to discuss this matter. Do not reply to this email. Call my office to make an appointment."

Alice sat and stared at the screen. She knew she hadn't done her best on the assignments, but she never dreamed she might be dismissed from the program. One of the unspoken policies of the college was that all grad students passed, and those in danger of failing, dropped out. It kept up the successful graduation completion ratings for the college. No one actually failed at the prestigious school. After several more minutes in front of her computer Alice slammed the power off button and watched the screen go dark, dying just like her plans for the future. What would she do with her life? Her mind reeled with possible scenarios, most of them frightening or sad. Maybe she could talk tomorrow with the one person she had met in the city who might give her advice. She set the alarm to awake in plenty of time to be at the park by ten o'clock. Angel said she would be there. Alice lay on her bed, fully clothed, and fell asleep.

32

DAY FIVE—FRIDAY NIGHT

BEA

Bea fell asleep while watching one of her favorite shows, N.C.I.S. New Orleans. She awoke to the sound of Sweetie's whines. The green glow of the digital clock displayed nine-thirty. Bea groaned and tried to reach Sweetie who lay on a small red and blue plaid doggie bed. Her arm dangled from the chair for a minute but she couldn't reach the little dog.

"What's wrong, Sweetie? Shhhhhh. Stop that whining. Bad dog. Shhhhhhhh." The pitiful sounds from Sweetie grew fainter and then stopped.

Bea switched channels to find another crime show. When she looked down at Sweetie, she knew something was terribly wrong. Sweetie panted; drool fell from his mouth; his eyes glazed over. Bea knelt beside him on the floor and tried to pick him up, but Sweetie yelped in pain. Bea hadn't taken Sweetie to the vet except for his regular yearly vaccinations. She calmly tried to think what to do. It was after hours for the regular vet's office, and the emergency animal facility was at least twenty blocks away. She'd need to call a cab. She couldn't carry him all that way, especially if he was in pain. There was no one, not one person, she could think to call to help her. She ransacked the apartment for a phone book and finally found it tucked under several stacks of magazines beside the kitchen table. After she called Ace Cab Company, she grabbed an old blanket from the closet and carefully wrapped up Sweetie, grabbed her purse, and left the apartment. As she walked down the hallway holding him as gently as she could, her neighbor's door cracked open slightly and she could see Mamie's shadowy figure backlit by the garish glow of her TV screen. "Something's wrong with my dog. I called a cab to take her to the emergency vet."

The fact that Bea told her neighbor what happened was not in character. Usually she kept to her own business and everyone else on the third floor kept to their own business, too. Bea suddenly realized that she forgot to write the address of the emergency facility. She knew the street, but not the number and giving a cabbie directions instead of an address could be a tricky matter. Evening cabbies often did not speak enough English for directions from a distraught pet owner.

“Could you help me?” she asked Mamie. This was not a question that Bea asked very often.

“What do you need?” asked the timid voice.

“Please look up the address of the emergency vet over on 60th Street. I need it for the cabbie.”

“Sure.” Mamie left her door open while she left to find the address. Bea worried that the cabbie had already arrived out front. Bea heard the woman rustling around inside and hoped she’d hurry. Mamie appeared at the door with a slip of paper in her hand.

“Here it is. Good luck. Let me know what happens. I like your little dog.”

Bea couldn’t have been more surprised at her neighbor’s comment.

“I thought you didn’t like dogs.”

“No, I mean it. I hope he’s OK. Come by tomorrow and let me know.”

**

At midnight Bea returned to the apartment without Sweetie. The experience at the emergency pet clinic took longer than she thought. The vet technician could not find anything obviously wrong, but she said Sweetie needed X-rays and blood tests. They would keep him overnight for observation. The young woman assured Bea that her pet was not in dire peril but there was some problem. Bea was handed a card showing a 3 p.m. appointment for the next day. The sympathetic tech called for her ride home so she would not have to try her luck hailing a cab at such a late hour.

Bea was tense on the ride back to the apartment even though the driver spoke perfect English with a British accent and seemed friendly enough for a foreigner. He told her he immigrated from the Bahamas and had been driving in the city for three years. Obviously he wanted to put her at ease but Bea was too upset to do more than nod and then politely pay the fare with a very small tip included. He did not act annoyed about the stingy tip and even smiled when she handed him the cash.

When Bea opened her front door, she felt a wave of loneliness sweep over her. It was the first time in five years she had been in the apartment alone. She sat down in the green plush recliner and wept.

Sweetie means everything to me. I can't live without him. I will be alone, totally alone. I have no one in my life but him. Bea's agony over Sweetie's possible loss felt like a giant hole opening in her chest. Fifteen minutes later when the tears finally stopped, Bea remembered she'd told Bounty she meet would her in the park tomorrow at ten. *How can I go without Sweetie?* Yet, going to the park seemed important. She hoped the time with Bounty would fill the day's hours until she could return for Sweetie's afternoon appointment. She needed a friend to tell what had happened. Bea wanted to believe that Bounty would understand and help her cope with her worry over Sweetie's emergency.

33

DAY FIVE—FRIDAY NIGHT

CAROL

The evening meal for Carol and her mom had been pleasant. They ordered take-out from their favorite Chinese place in the next block. Carol begged for the Sweet and Sour Chicken and her mom ordered two egg rolls, two wonton soups, and extra fried brown rice. The television was not on as it always was when her dad was there. They talked about her school without being told to be quiet for the latest breaking news. Carol really missed her dad, but Mom hardly spoke of him after the first few days. In the last week, however, she had acted tense and worried. After they put the empty food cartons in the trash, Carol's mom asked her to sit on the sofa, holding out her arms to her. She wanted Carol to sit close and give her a big hug. Carol sensed that a serious talk was coming.

"Carol, we need to talk. This is going to be hard for both of us."

"Sure, Mom. What is it? Are we moving?"

"Yes, honey. I have no choice but to move us to a cheaper place. It's out of your school district but I'll apply for a transfer so you can stay at P.S. 236. I want you to stay there until the end of this school year."

Carol didn't look at her mom. She tried not to cry by squeezing her fists together as hard as she could—so hard that her fingernails dug into her palms and hurt.

"Don't you have anything to ask me?" said her mom with a hint of hope in her voice.

"Wouldn't make any difference, would it?" was Carol's sullen reply.

"No, I guess not. I don't think I'll get a raise at work this year. Since Dad left I can't afford this rent anymore."

"Is he coming back? Ever?"

"Don't know about that. He wouldn't say where he was. He's getting his retirement checks now, I guess. Try to understand, Carol, we can't stay here. Our budget is very tight."

"What's the other place like? Do we have to share a bathroom down the hall with somebody else?" Carol knew a girl at school who said that's what she and her mother did in their apartment building.

"Oh no. We'll have our own bath in the apartment. But it's a lot smaller, or maybe I should say cozy for us."

"Cozy? As in really small, huh?"

"Yes," her mom sighed.

"Is there room for a table to do my homework and drawings for art class?"

"There's plenty of room for a table. Carol, let's make this our adventure."

"Adventure? That's supposed to be fun. Moving to a new place doesn't sound fun to me. I really want to stay at my school. How many more blocks to walk?"

"It's fifteen blocks away from here. The building is pretty nice, and we'll have a second floor flat. Not many stairs to climb."

"Can I still go to the park?"

"Sure, honey, we can go to the park on the weekends."

"No, Mom. I mean go to the park after school."

"I don't let you do that now. But we can go together on the weekends like I said."

"You didn't understand what I told you. I've gone to the park every day after school and I want to keep going. I'm old enough to go by myself."

Her mom looked very surprised at Carol's revelation.

"Carol, I've told you about dangers of a young girl alone. You don't have my permission to go to the park after school. Not now, and not in the foreseeable future."

"Why do you use those words...in the foreseeable future, Mom? You should say what you mean! You mean never! So say it that way. And I'm old enough to go alone. No one bothers me in the park. It's like I'm invisible."

"We're not discussing this anymore, Carol. Things are hard enough for us now. I won't have you disobeying me. You're to come home directly after school every day and keep the doors locked until I get home! Do you understand?"

"I heard what you said. But, I'm going to the park and you can't stop me! You'll be at work. Besides, if I don't go back to the park I might fail art. That's where I have been after school every day this week doing my art assignments." Carol's defiance was clear.

Carol's mom had tears in her eyes, tears of frustration. "What else are you keeping from me that you've been doing?"

"Nothing! Nothing else!" Carol shouted. Carol's angry reaction to her mom was not typical. Her face turned beet red and she rolled her eyes upward in despair. "Uh... sorry, I yelled."

"Carol, I think you're lying to me. Go to your room right now!"

"You sound like Dad. You're raising your voice. You didn't like it when Dad did it to you."

"No, I didn't like it when he yelled at me. And it's a good thing he's gone." Her mom's voice cracked with emotion.

"Good for you, but not good for me. It's not good having to move right in the middle of school," was the subdued reply from Carol.

Carol felt a terrible ache in her stomach and folded her arms tightly in front of her belly.

"Honey, let's stop this conversation. We're both upset. In the morning after I get back from market we'll talk again. We need to help each other, Carol. It's the two of us now."

Carol didn't say another word but went to her

room and closed the door quietly. She told herself she wouldn't cry, but she started crying so hard her chest hurt. She vowed to herself she'd go to the park while her mom was out at the market. Nothing would stop her from keeping her promise to Charity. She'd be there at ten. That's what she would do. She needed to see her new friend who told the stories. Carol began to recall each story and to think what lesson she might learn. She would ask Charity more about the stories tomorrow.

34

DAY SIX—SATURDAY MORNING

ALICE

Alice's alarm went off at six as usual. She had forgotten to reset it later for Saturday. Once awakened by the insistent buzzer, she tried to return to sleep, but thoughts of getting to the park by ten o'clock kept her awake. After she consumed two cups of coffee and the remains of a stale bagel, Alice paced around the apartment. After a few seconds she turned on her computer. She read again the email from her professor and the last assignment she turned in. *Yes, half-heartedly done and not good work. Can't do any better and don't want to try.* The decision to drop out of school was momentous and weighed on her like the elephant that sat on people's chests in TV commercials for asthma medication *What should I do? Leave this all totally behind?* She couldn't think of a good solution.

Not wanting to be too early to meet Angel, Alice decided to take an hour's jog starting at eight-thirty. She first ran on the sidewalks surrounding the park. Alice was tempted to go straight to where she hoped Angel waited but once in the park she decided to run past the gravel path and turn around only in time to arrive at the bench exactly at ten. Even if everything else about her life in the city and school were falling apart, she could keep herself on her routine. *Wait a minute*, she thought. *I could arrive at the bench a half hour early. I'd see from which direction Angel comes. She must live close to the park and doesn't walk too far. Angel's much too frail for a long walk.*

Alice kept to her new plan. She jogged around the perimeter of the park on the main avenue along the river.

After she made the turn by the boat dock, she ran at a brisker pace on the path, soon finding herself away from the river and in the center of the park. Since she came from a different direction, the park looked unfamiliar. She never thought about seeing the same features of the park but observing them from the south side first. Ahead she could see a faint outline of the pagoda, but she hadn't come to the gravel path. Once on the little path she slowed to a steady walk, struggling to get her breathing under control. She felt winded today. All the stress of the upcoming appointment with Professor Martinez weighed on her mind.

As she rounded the bend in the path she saw the empty iron bench. She stood on the grass close to the pagoda and waited for Angel to arrive. If she sat on the bench she might not be able to observe her arrival. She stood for a long moment watching some pigeons land on the roof. The entrance to the pagoda seemed to be luring her inside. As her eyes adjusted to the dim light, she realized she stood in a very dusty room with exposed rafters hung with bedraggled spider webs. An empty pile of twigs that might have once been a small bird's nest rested in one corner. *What happened to the beautiful blue painted ceiling? Did I imagine it?* Never had she been as confused as at that moment. Her memory of the blue ceiling was clear—she hadn't dreamed it. She'd seen it on Monday, only five days earlier. Anxious and perplexed, Alice turned to look out the door and to her surprise two women sat on the iron bench. Such strange things could be happening. Angel sat beside a large older woman with a very unusual hairdo. Alice had never seen someone that age with so many pink and red ribbons tied on small tight braids. The two were engaged in a serious conversation. A wave of resentment wasn't what she expected, but that's what she felt when she saw Angel talking to someone else. *Angel said she'd meet me! Who is that woman? No one was there just a minute ago.*

As a further complication of her conflicted feelings, Alice noticed a young girl sat on one of the low walls farther down the path. The girl held a large sketch pad and intently watched Angel and the strange woman on the bench. The realization came to her that the girl was drawing them. The two women on the bench did not appear to have seen Alice standing inside the entrance of the pagoda. Likewise, the women paid no attention to the young girl on the wall. There had never been anyone else in this area of the park except for Angel for five days. *What are these people doing here?* Alice felt disconnected from what she saw right in front of her. The black woman, dressed in an outlandishly loud flowered housedress, arose from the bench and started walking away sadly shaking her head. After about ten steps, she turned and waved at Angel but Angel did not respond.

When the woman walked out of sight, the girl got up from her position on the wall and began to slowly walk toward the bench. She held the pad in her hand. A beaming smile radiated from her face. Alice watched Angel reach for her grey umbrella, her usual routine. The smiling child approached the bench and held out the sketch pad to Angel. An earnest conversation between the two began.

Alice feared she was trapped in a disturbingly surreal dream. She could see everyone else, but no one seemed to see her. Suddenly, panic struck her so hard that she thought she might pass out. She stepped back into the shaded interior of the pagoda and sat on the dusty floor. She kept her back to the entrance and stared at the floor. Time seemed to stand still for her inside the pagoda. Trying to make sense of the scene outside, Alice sat down with her knees pulled to her chest and listened to her own ragged breaths.

35

DAY SIX—SATURDAY MORNING

BEA

Bea slept fitfully until six thirty. When she awoke Sweetie was not whining at her bedside and the jolt of the memory of what happened during the night swept over her. She'd never felt so alone in her life. *He's just a dog. Dogs get sick. Dogs don't live as long as humans. Dogs die.* Bea couldn't accept any of the things she kept trying to tell herself. She wanted to get through the first part of the day and go to the park as always. Only today it would be earlier since Bounty had told her to arrive at ten. Bea needed Bounty's sympathy for Sweetie's situation. After she made a pot of Earl Grey tea and boiled two eggs in a dented white enamel pan, she poured the tea, ate the eggs, and tried hard not think about Sweetie.

Completely out of character, she went to the phone and dialed the number of her neighbor down the hall. Then she remembered the hour and hung up before there was an answer. She didn't like early calls and her neighbor probably didn't either. The phone immediately rang back.

"Bea, did you call me just now?"

"Yes. I'm sorry it's so early. I didn't get back last night until midnight."

"Did your dog die?"

"No, he's at the vet clinic for some tests. I can't pick him up until this afternoon."

"Well, fine. Hope he gets better. Will you come by for coffee on Monday? The super has been up to his tricks pretending he did repairs to the laundry room. We need to talk."

"I don't want to talk about the super. I'll come by Monday if my Sweetie doesn't die." Bea's abrupt reply was met with a long silence.

"Hope he doesn't. See you Monday then." The line went dead and the early morning neighborly conversation ended.

Bea fussed around the apartment for as long as she could. She arranged pillows on the sofa, stacked magazines, and dusted the collection of salt and pepper shakers in a small display cabinet. By quarter after nine she'd done everything she could think of to keep herself busy and make the time pass. She planned to arrive earlier than ten o'clock as she had promised Bounty. Maybe she would see the path Bounty walked to come into the park. She felt a sense of urgency to talk with Bounty about Sweetie. She wondered if Bounty would try to tell her that the stories were a lesson for her in the midst of such a personally unsettling event. The stories were only fanciful stories, but this was reality for Bea.

Bea arrived at the iron bench at nine forty, only to find Bounty already sitting there as usual; but for the first time she did not have her bags of bread for the pigeons. There were no birds in sight. Instead, Bounty had brought a grey umbrella that lay open on the ground beside her. How strange, Bea thought. The skies are clear. No rain forecast.

"Where's your little dog, Bea?" Bounty asked with obvious concern. Bea without her Sweetie meant something was wrong.

"Something's happened to him. I took him to the emergency pet clinic last night. I'm afraid I might lose him."

"Don't worry. I know how upset you are right now. I promise you he'll be fine."

"I want to believe that'll be true, just like I want to

believe your stories about your mamá. I'm not sure I can."

"Maybe you don't like the lessons my stories are teaching you. What have my stories been about? Do you remember them all?"

"A unicorn that saved your mamá—a flood that drowned some chickens—a long trip to see family—a frog who was not a frog but a person—a storyteller in the circus. I remember them all."

"Have any of the stories made you ask yourself about your life? I do not make up stories. My stories are lessons." Bounty's demeanor was more serious than Bea had ever seen her in the past days.

A tugboat horn sounded and as Bea turned toward the sound from the river, she noticed a young girl sitting on the low vine-covered wall down the path.

"What's that kid doing by herself at this time of day?" Bea's indignant question made Bounty turn with a look of surprise.

"I think she is drawing pictures. She's fine. Don't be bothered."

"Never been anyone else around when we are here."

"Today is different, no? Now, you can tell me what lessons you have learned from the stories." Bounty's insistence bothered Bea.

"That kid doesn't even act like she knows we are here. She's really intent on her drawing."

"That's not a lesson from my stories I told you. The kid, as you say, is waiting to talk to me. She doesn't like being called a kid. " Bounty's voice was tinged with impatience for once.

"You know her? Well, ask her over here to sit with us. Have you told her your stories?"

"*Si,* I have told her stories…but, *it*'s not the right time to talk with her now. Tell me what you have learned. You're never too old to learn, Bea."

"I'll tell you what I think. Your stories are about your mamá appreciating what she had. She was protected and later loved. She found a treasure when she wasn't expecting it. I guess she knew how to enjoy life. I know I've got it right…about the stories, I mean." Bea's answers sounded like she knew she understood the lessons.

"Do you enjoy life like my mamá? Why aren't you happy, my friend? Sweetie is everything to you, I know. But, you need more in your life, Bea. Think more about the stories and learn to be happy. Who can you help and make happy? That's what I came to tell you today. And one more thing, Bea, the stories are over."

"You won't tell me more stories next week? I like coming here to see you."

"You have the stories for a lifetime. I'll go to new place. I won't be here again. *Te deseo mucha felicidad.* I wish you much happiness."

"So that's it? You're saying good-bye? I won't see you again?" asked Bea. A sense of loss overwhelmed her.

"*Vaya con dios,*" said Bounty smiling at Bea. "We part as friends. You'll now start a new time of your life, a happy time."

Bounty reached down and picked up the grey umbrella, a tender look on her smiling face. A few dried leaves from the maple tree nearby fluttered to the ground when she snapped the umbrella shut.

Bea slowly walked away from the bench. After about ten steps, she looked back and waved at Bounty one last time. As she turned back around, she noticed the young girl had left her place on the wall. With her drawing pad under her arm, she approached the old bench, sat down. She began swinging her legs back and forth as young kids sometimes do when they are waiting for something to happen. Bounty walked in the other direction, her white skirt whipped around by a sudden light breeze. She swung the grey umbrella from side to side. A small white pigeon circled and flapped around the top of the pagoda and then landed on the grass. The bird waddled slowly as a hungry pigeon does when expecting a kind person to throw a few bread crumbs on the ground. Bounty never looked at the pigeon.

36

DAY SIX—SATURDAY MORNING

CAROL

Carol made a point of setting her wind-up alarm clock for eight o'clock. The morning light shone through the two broken blinds on her bedroom window waking her up just before the alarm went off. The smell of coffee brewing in the kitchen meant that her mom's routine for the day had already started. She'd probably already made her list for the market. It was a six block twenty minute walk to the market that had the best sales counting all the stoplights and street crossings. Her mom took about two hours at the market since she checked and double-checked all sales coupons and ads. The walk back was always slower as there were a couple of more stops on the way home at the newsstand or the bakery for some special bagels for their lunches. Carol decided that she would have close to two hours in the park to be with Charity. Her mom would never know she was out of the apartment. She would leave as soon as her mom left and then return in time to be waiting in the kitchen to help her unpack the cart full of groceries. She hoped her mom's departure to the market would be close to nine-thirty.

"Good morning, honey. Did you sleep well? Lots of sirens last night."

"I didn't hear them."

Carol took the box of granola cereal from the cabinet and poured herself a large bowl.

"Do you like that granola? I'll buy more if it's on sale."

Everything had to be on sale or her mom wouldn't buy it.

"Whatever you find on sale is fine. Will you get some apples for my lunch?"

"Carol, do you want to talk about last night?"

"Let's wait 'til later in the day. I know we'll be moving soon. I need to get over being sad about it."

"Good girl. I knew I could count on you. Most mothers aren't so lucky."

Carol liked being called "good girl," but she also

knew it was her mom's way to smooth things over.

"How about going to market with me this morning? We could stop for a pretzel from the cart on the corner of 45th. Your favorite!"

"I've got to finish up my art project for Monday. I have math and science homework, too. And, I need to read twenty more pages of a book for English class."

"That sounds like a lot of homework for one weekend. Have you been turning in your work or is it make-up time?"

"It's the regular stuff we have for every weekend. I've got an extra art assignment. I need to draw some people's faces."

"So what's the book you need to read?"

"The book? Oh...it's about a bunch of really mean boys who are on an island."

"Lord of the Flies"? They're still requiring that book? I read that in high school, not middle school."

"Maybe my generation's more advanced. Just joking, Mom. It's a gross book. One of the boys is called Piggy, but you knew that. Mr. Brown always assigns books about boys."

"Well, that doesn't seem right. Oh, honey, I may go on to market a little early. I made the list already. It's eight-thirty now. I will probably be back no later than eleven or so."

"Oh, Mom...uh, don't leave so early. You could drink another cup of coffee and I'll sort out the laundry for us to do later. You never leave before nine-fifteen. You won't miss any sales." Carol tried to think of other delaying tactics. The timing and her plans for the park were not working out as she had hoped.

"Thanks for offering to sort the laundry, but I thought you were ready to start homework. I'll finish up this cup and get an early start. We'll do the laundry when I get back. Be sure the door is locked behind me."

Carol looked at the kitchen clock displaying the time as her mom went out the door. She would have to be very careful to return from the park no later than eleven-fifteen. That did not leave much time to see Charity starting at ten, but she was not going to miss the time with Charity. Carol wanted to tell her friend about her move away from the neighborhood. Most of all she wanted to talk about how hard it would be to change schools. Besides, she needed to think about the stories and ask which one had a lesson for the problem of moving away. Every one of Charity's stories had a lesson for her, but she needed Charity to help her understand it.

Carol timed her arrival on the dot at ten just as she had promised Charity. To her disappointment, someone else occupied the bench they'd shared all week. A middle-aged black woman with an unusual hairdo of small braids wrapped with pink and red ribbons sat on the bench in the mid-morning sun. She appeared to be talking to herself. Carol had never seen anyone else around this part of the park, but then it was Saturday morning, not a regular weekday afternoon.

Carol sat down on the low stone wall a bit down the path by a clump of trees where she hoped she wouldn't draw any attention. She'd seen street people muttering to themselves. Her mom had told her never to make contact with such people because it usually meant they were a little off, meaning slightly crazy. She pulled her drawing pad from her backpack and decided to try a portrait of the black woman. It would make a good picture and would show Miss Brandt that she observed different people. She thought the woman's look was eccentric and rather interesting, too. This would be her first drawing for today. *The funny woman will be my first drawing today. Then I'll try another of the pagoda.* She looked over to across the path toward the pagoda and noticed a jogger stood in front looking up at a flock of pigeons on the roof. *That jogger by the pagoda will be my second drawing. I can remember how pretty that looks.* To her amazement, Carol watched the jogger duck inside the pagoda, disappearing into the shadows. *Very odd things are happening today. The park seems crowded with two strangers. They are both acting weird.* Turning her attention to the woman on the bench, she began to draw.

The woman continued to talk to herself and even gestured a few times as if talking to an imaginary friend. Once Carol completed the portrait of the heavy-set black woman, she turned the page in her sketch book and outlined the pagoda with a thick black pencil. From memory she drew the jogger who had stood with her back to Carol. *Not my best work. Needs color. I'll work on it more later.*

With relief she saw the large woman with the ribbon hairdo stand and leave the bench. She hadn't looked in Carol's direction. As Carol gathered up her backpack and prepared to walk across the grass, the woman suddenly turned and gave a little wave in the direction of the bench. Carol thought to herself the woman looked very sad like she was saying good bye forever to someone, only there was no one there. Her mom would have said this proved the woman was a mentally off; but, the little wave made Carol think that sometimes a person might want to say good-bye to a place like the beautiful iron bench.

Carrying her pad under her arm, she settled on the bench and waited impatiently for Charity to arrive. She swung her legs in rhythm and hummed a song to herself. In the distance toward the pagoda she could see a figure backlit by the sun walking down the path. *Charity! She came like she promised!* As she got closer, Carol noticed Charity carrying a grey umbrella, gently swinging it back and forth. *How very strange. It's a sunny day. No rain clouds. Why did Charity bring an umbrella?*

"Hey, Charity. I was here right on time, but you're late. Did you oversleep?"

"Nope. Talking to someone. Had to finish that conversation first."

"Well, someone else was here first but then she left. A woman I had never seen before. There's usually no one here in the afternoons when we come."

"Yeah, I know. That's how it's supposed to be. One listener, one storyteller, one story. It's simpler that way. Do you get it?"

"I'm not sure...but look! Here's a picture I drew of her while I waited for you." Carol shoved the drawing toward Charity with pride.

"Looks just like her," said Charity as she smiled.

"How would you know? Do you think my picture is good or not?"

"Like I said, it looks just like Bea." Charity emphasized the words "just like" emphatically.

"Do you know her?"

"Uh...someone that looks like her should be named Bea. How's that for my answer?"

"Well, answer me this, please. Why are you carrying that old umbrella? Looks like it came out of the dumpster. It's not raining. And, it's not your style." Carol's voice rose as if she was slightly angry. While Carol spoke, Charity had opened the umbrella and placed it on the ground by the bench. She carefully brushed away some dead leaves around her feet so they wouldn't drift into the umbrella's upturned canopy.

"It's my style. My favorite possession. Anyway, are you upset this morning, Carol?

"Yeah, I am. I need to talk to you before you start today's story." Carol felt deflated and sad about what she had to tell Charity.

"What's up with you, kid? Don't look at me like that. I like to call you kid. I mean it in a nice way."

"My mom and I have to move away. Pretty far

from the park. I might have trouble meeting you after school." Carol's voice broke and tears welled up in her eyes.

"You'll remember our stories and can keep telling them to yourself. That way you won't forget the lessons. You do remember the stories, don't you?"

"I liked the one about the circus and the storyteller the best. The last one from yesterday. It reminded me of meeting you and how it changed a lot of stuff for me." Carol sighed.

"Name the other stories and tell me what they meant to you."

"Is this a test or something?"

"Just want to be sure you remember them all."

Carol was glad she had recalled all the stories while she walked to the park. "One about a unicorn that saved your grandmother from being killed with her family. Really sad. In fact, they're all about your grandmother."

"Go on." Charity nodded and seemed pleased with Carol's response.

"Another story was about a person named Frog who helped catch a thief. That was day before yesterday. Your grandmother was in that one, too. On Tuesday one about finding a treasure after all the pigs got killed in the flood. That was a good one because she found a treasure and had a better life."

"And the other one?"

"Oh yeah, the long trip your grandmother took to meet her family. It had no ending. I wanted to know how it turned out."

"Maybe, you don't always know how things will turn out, but it doesn't mean it will be a bad ending. Could be for the best, you know."

"Are you trying to tell me that moving away might be a good thing for me?"

"No, but it might not be a bad thing, either."

"I dunno. I'm really sad." Carol wanted Charity to show her sympathy. She didn't want to hear that moving away might be a good thing for her.

"The lessons from the stories were for you. I know you'll remember them. Changes in your life are what you make them. You have a whole wonderful life ahead, Carol. You will change and it'll be good for you. But, the two of us will have to make some changes, too."

"Why would we make changes? You sound like there won't be any more stories! I'll be here until the end of the month for sure. Our rent is paid up until then."

"Well, Carol, I won't be here anymore. I have to move on, too. You'll find happiness with your amazing talent. Your art will bring you a good life. You have the stories. You don't need anything else."

Charity bent down and began to close the grey umbrella.

"Wait! You can't leave! I have to draw another picture of you. My teacher said to do another one." Carol had tears rolling down her cheeks. "It won't take long. Please. I don't want to ever forget you."

"You showed my picture to your teacher?"

"Please, please, let me draw another one if this is the last...our last time here." Carol wiped her tears. "I have to make this the best one I've ever done."

Charity sat very still in the bright morning sun as Carol drew on her pad. After ten long minutes of silence except for the soft scratching of Carol's pencil, she closed the pad and said, "Thanks. It's done."

Carol smiled and radiated contentment like a lovely warm puppy held close to the heart. She felt happier than she had in a long time.

"Won't you let me see?" Charity peered over at the pad Carol held.

"Nope. Sorry, but you can't see it. I'll always remember you just like you are today and what I've learned from you."

"Carol, remember the stories and don't be afraid

of change."

"I won't be afraid. Thanks for helping me understand that I can be brave, just like your grandmother. I'm glad she told you the stories. Thanks for being my friend."

Charity leaned over and gave Carol a long hug. She picked up the open umbrella and closed it after shaking out a few leaves that had been blown inside. She turned to Carol and said, "See you, kid." They both smiled. Carol watched as Charity walked up the path toward the pagoda, twirled the folded umbrella in her left hand and hummed to herself. Tears blinded Carol momentarily and when she wiped them away, Charity was gone.

37

DAY SIX—SATURDAY MORNING

THE STORYTELLER

Alice sat in the pagoda until she could not wait another minute there. The dust tickled her nose and the musty smells sickened her. When she looked at her watch, she was amazed that an hour had passed. She had dozed off and felt disoriented upon awakening. She remembered she'd ducked inside the pagoda to hide from what she'd seen—Angel conversing with a large black woman and a young girl in the distance bent over a sketch pad. *Why were others in my special place in the park? I need some comfort from Angel today. I've never been so uncertain about my life.* The alarming thought struck her that perhaps Angel had left while she slept. She emerged from the pagoda and looked toward the bench. A wave of relief swept over her. Angel sat primly on the bench, the grey umbrella open on the ground beside her. Her eyes were closed and she swayed slightly like she was singing to herself.

Alice found herself running across the grassy area to the bench. Her pounding footsteps startled Angel.

"Why, Alice. Good morning. Did you run past the pagoda and back this morning? I didn't see you pass."

"I was in the pagoda. I've been here since before ten."

"And why would you be in the pagoda all that time? Why didn't you come to sit with me?"

"Angel, strange things have happened this morning. I saw other people here with you. I thought you were here to meet me this morning." Alice's voice sounded unsteady.

"Do you mean Bea and Carol? Did their presence upset you?"

"So I did not imagine them?"

"No, my dear, they were listeners, too. Others who needed stories like you. They saw who they needed at the time."

"Saw who they needed? Please explain. I'm really confused."

"Not everyone saw the same storyteller, but they needed the same stories."

"I don't know what you mean about seeing the same storyteller. You're the storyteller. Isn't that what you do? Tell stories to people?" Alice paused for a moment and tried to find the words to express how she felt. "I have never met anyone like you, Angel. Something unexplainable seems to have happened."

"Stories may need explanation but not always. I came to you first. Only you saw me for who I am. The others needed someone else. You will understand one day. Well, now, can you explain what the stories have meant for you?"

"Wait a minute. What do you mean I saw you for who you are?"

"You can ponder that question on your own time. You will eventually understand. The point is, can you tell me about the stories? What have you learned?"

"You want me to recite the stories back to you?" Alice's mind was raced with details of the five stories she'd heard in the last five days.

"No, no. Tell me the themes and how you understood what I was teaching you in the stories."

"Oh. Well, there was the first one about a unicorn, which, by the way, I didn't believe. Or, I mean, I didn't believe there was a unicorn, but maybe you saw something that day. Whatever happened you were spared being killed with your family. Then you had to make another life. Another one was about a long journey you took with your father. I think it was about searching for family and repairing relationships. That one did not have a satisfactory ending."

"Do all stories have to have a satisfactory ending as you say?" Angel's questions were like probes, making Alice think more deeply about her answers. "That's only two. There were more. Please, go on."

"Angel, this is odd. Why are you wanting me to retell you the topics of your own stories? Are you testing me? And, by the way, some of the stories seemed to have happened a long, long time ago. How old are you, anyway?"

Angel chuckled out loud when Alice threw in the question about her age.

"Again, not important for you to know. You can imagine whatever age you wish. Yes, the test is that you understand and can retell the lessons to others who might need them. So, please, finish telling me about my other stories."

From the look on Angel's face, Alice realized she had endless patience.

"Of course, that's what I should do. Well, one

story was long and rather complicated about a person called Frog who was falsely accused of being a thief. That story that puzzled me. At least the Madame told the truth at the end."

"Oh. Alice, maybe you need to think more about wrongly judging people and their true character. That was a major lesson of the story."

"If you put it that way. I guess I've misjudged people in my life." Alice nodded seriously.

"Yes, that's the way I put it, as you say. What an unusual way to say that you acknowledge the lesson." Angel shook her head as if disappointed that Alice did not completely understand the whole lesson from the frog story.

"Let's see...another one was about when you found a treasure after the poor cows drowned in a flood."

"Which was more important—the cows, the treasure, or the flood?" Angel's comments were abstract concepts, not just a simple story.

"I think the lesson for me was about finding something valuable even after a disaster." Alice looked expectantly, hoping for an affirmation from Angel.

"Very good, Alice. Other lessons in that story, too. They will come to you as you mature."

"And the last one you told me yesterday about a circus and finding someone who changed your life. I got that one right away. Meeting a special person in unusual circumstances can change your life. Like meeting you here in the park!"

"Yes! Very good, my dear. You have understood many of the lessons. You will understand more when you spend time recalling the stories again and again. Your future will be changed by what you have learned. Excellent!"

"Angel, I know I have much more to learn from you."

"Well, my dear, I have finished my time with you." Angel exuded her approval of what Alice had said about the stories.

"You've finished your time with me? Five stories change my future? Aren't you coming back to the park again?" A stunned look flooded over Alice's face.

"Three good questions, Alice. The answer to the first two questions is "yes." I think you understand what the answer to your last question is. You have a calling to continue the stories as I have. You won't fulfill that calling for quite some time, but you will someday. Follow your heart and tell stories, my dear girl. Follow your heart and tell stories."

Angel leaned over to pick up the grey umbrella.

As she brushed two small crisp leaves that had stuck under the opened canopy, she commented, “Always a few remains from stories that can’t be completely explained, like these leaves that catch in the umbrella every day.” With a loud snap, she closed the umbrella.

When she handed the grey umbrella to Alice, Angel had a beatific look. “For you to use in your future, my dear.”

Angel rose from the bench, straightened her clothing and took a few moments to rearrange her little purple hat. She crossed the path and walked toward the pagoda. There appeared to be two other people standing there. One might have been a woman in white and the other could have been a slender younger person, but Alice couldn’t be sure. The sun glinted off of the metal roof of the pagoda in a blinding blaze. She raised her left hand to shield her eyes, but she could not see what she thought was there. Alice gripped the grey umbrella and stood by the bench, the autumn sun warm on her shoulders. Not a cloud in sight.

THE END OF THE BEGINNING.

THE BEGINNING AGAIN

Years later, once upon a time, no, it will be thrice upon a time because the story is again about three people learning about the magic of storytelling. Once one has a magical experience, two things can happen. The first is that one will dismiss what happened as some fleeting illusion of the mind. The second is that one learns and can recognize the magic when it returns. These experiences don't happen every day—not every year—perhaps only once or twice in a lifetime. One must be aware when it happens.

38

THE AUTHOR

The young author sat in the expensive red leather chair in her publisher's office and waited for the inner door to open. A magnificent view of the park and the river was ten floors below. She looked for the tugboats and sailboats that made their watery paths with swirling wakes. To her disappointment, none were to be seen today. As a lone Coast Guard patrol boat went slowly downstream about its daily business, the image came to her of a serious businessman entering a large office building in order to "make a living", as the old saying went. *Was it called "making a living" when it was a job one hated? Was it termed "a career" if one loved the work?* Her thoughts often wandered off into inexplicable twists once she got caught on a phrase or word that intrigued her. Images she saw would remind her of other images and there was no stopping the way she could keep relating sights and sounds to other sights and sounds. *I am happy so I must have a career. A career in writing. Never would have believed it ten years ago. Glad I followed my heart.*

Over the last ten years, Marilee Mason had written three successful historical novels. She'd found a popular niche writing about 20th century feminists, their influences and their various loves. The reading public was mostly interested in their love life and sexual escapades. The two years spent taking creative writing classes at City College after she dropped out of the Graduate Institute for Urban Planning had been the right choice.

With a comfortable bank account from her successes, she'd recently moved into a larger apartment uptown with her little dog Sweetie Pie. Her friends teased her about naming a male dog such a silly name. She couldn't give an explanation other than she'd had a crazy dream about a cute mutt with such a name before she adopted him from the shelter. Her appointment today with Stephanie Culpepper was to discuss her recent failure to meet a first deadline for a new historical novel. The ideas were not flying onto the paper; no, they were flying all over the room and out the windows. Surely, she was too young and too clever to have writer's block.

The door burst open and a tall thin woman rushed in. Her red frizzed hair flew in all directions and her gold rimmed bifocals were askew on her freckled nose. She was a study in frantic motion. As she tossed a large purse toward a wooden chair several items fell out, but she didn't appear to notice. She slapped a large brown envelope, the kind that usually contained bulky manuscripts from aspiring writers, down onto the large oak desk.

"Good morning, Alice. I do prefer your real first name. Marilee Mason is such a pretentious nom de plume. You look a little down. Not feeling well? Please don't give me the flu if that's what you have. Did you wash your hands before you came?" Stephanie was known for her germ phobia but she was also known to mentor many young writers through agonizing times in their careers. Most she had saved but some she had not. Alice hoped to be one of the saved ones.

"I can't do this one. The ideas aren't coming. I'm distracted. I don't want to be known for three good novels and then a crummy fourth one that limps along like a lazy dog trying to find a shady place and lick its butt."

"Well, that's quite an image of self-loathing. You're surely not at that point, Alice."

"Help me, Stephanie. I'm a writer. I'm called to do this crazy thing. Why do I feel this way?"

"Look, Alice. I'm your publisher now. I was your first editor before I started the company and before that I think I was your friend. I can still remember meeting for coffee at the student center before we both had any idea what we would do with our lives."

"Those were the days, all right. We both didn't have a clue except that I hated urban planning and you wanted a Ph.D in English but didn't see a career path. Steph, do you have any great ideas now?"

"I've given this situation some thought. You're young enough to publish in a different genre. What would you say trying your hand with children's stories?"

"Hmmmm. I feel rather uncomfortable around children. Is there a special reason you think children's literature would be best for me at this point in my career?" After she said it, the absurdity of the comment hung in the air for a moment before it evaporated, just like her ideas had vanished inexplicably for the new novel.

"Hey girlfriend, many aspiring writers try different approaches. Talent is talent. You have talent. Please consider it. I'm thinking older mature children who read above their grade level. Smart kids need good literature, but also need lessons."

Alice was not one to make spur of the moment decisions yet she felt a wave of hope pour through her very being. Stephanie's ideas about what would catch on in the world of literature had been a bonanza to other clients. A new challenge to craft stories that would teach and entertain older children was not something she would have ever dreamed of doing. She loved the idea.

"Well, why not? I don't need to put off a decision. Just tell me where to start on this new project. Oh no, wait! Children's books are illustrated, and I can't draw a decent circle."

"Don't be silly. I'm not asking you to write and illustrate. I'll put out a few feelers for an illustrator. Books like what I have in mind would call for a special type of art work. We can review a few portfolios. Now you start thinking of a theme. Actually, four to five small stories in a series often works very well."

Stephanie's tone was upbeat as she started to pace about the room. "Yes, yes! This could be perfect for you. You imagine all kinds of possibilities and you see things that no one else notices. Just like a curious kid. The other day when we were cutting though the park you said you could visualize what the park would have looked like a century ago. That sort of thinking, Alice. Those ideas would translate to good stories for your new audience."

Stephanie's enthusiasm caught Alice by surprise. She wanted to be up to the job and not disappoint her mentor and friend.

"What about the deadline for the historical novel? Can you fix that?"

"Of course, remember my triple personality—editor, publisher and friend. I can fix anything. You just write, dear author."

39

THE ARTIST

Stephanie Culpepper looked over the list of well-known illustrators and several aspiring artists, unknowns but with interesting resumes. After narrowing down the list, she was left with three possibilities. One, a well-known elderly gentleman, often took six months to complete his sketches. She wasn't sure he would live long enough to see the project through, especially if there were several books in the series. Alice's new undertaking might last five to six years, if successful. The second was a moderately successful artist used by two different publishers for graphic science fiction novels. Graphic novels sold like hotcakes in many areas of the country, but not exactly the genre she had in mind for this project. The last name on the list was C.J. McGinnis whose resume was light. Art education credentials were impressive, but apparently the artist hadn't been hired by any author, major or minor. There were two excellent recommendation letters from the art school director, and a nature magazine editor. The artist had submitted several illustrations of endangered animals. Stephanie wanted to see the portfolio and had the feeling that an unknown would be prompt with submissions.

After email exchanges, Stephanie knew she could expect a package of sample work within two weeks. Her suggested deadline, the first Monday of next month, gave plenty of time for a review with Alice before a meeting. Stephanie wanted to keep Alice to the new submission deadlines.

**

The UPS box filled with illustrations arrived exactly on time one afternoon when Alice sat in the offices of Culpepper Publishing. She'd come to pick up Stephanie for coffee and conversation. Three days before Alice had submitted two proposals for her new theme and wanted to hear Stephanie's critique in person.

"My, my, look what's arrived, Alice. The submission from our unknown illustrator. I would love to make another young person famous, so let's see what's here." Stephanie relished her role as benefactor and mentor.

"That's what I love about you, Stephanie. Your humility!" Alice laughed.

Stephanie carefully opened the box and began to spread the sketches out on the large mahogany table. Alice peered over at the papers and gasped. The look on her face was one of utter disbelief.

"Who is this artist? I don't have the words. How can this be?"

"Well, I agree these are amazingly beautiful. I asked for three portraits, a few animals, a couple of architectural drawings and then anything else to show off originality and talent. Nice that color, ink, and charcoal were done for the presentation."

"You don't understand, Steph. These are people and places I've seen before. I don't understand. You must contact this person immediately for a meeting."

"You can't be serious! You know the women in these portraits? This is one crazy coincidence. The name is C.J. McGinnis, graduate of a prestigious art school, two impressive recommendations, but no real success in the field yet."

"That's all the information you have? How about a photo?"

"Nope, didn't ask for that. Could be taken for discrimination. I always try to be neutral in previewing unknowns." Stephanie covered her bases in the hiring process. "Why would C.J. McGinnis send portraits of people you know? Who are these people?"

"It's hard to explain. I've seen this black woman one time—at a distance. She is pretty unforgettable with all those red and pink ribbons in her hair. This one looks like a young girl I saw one morning in the park but never met. This one is me!"

"The one of a figure looking at a pagoda? You can't even see the person's face or tell if it's male or female. You are imagining all this, correct? Writers have such imagination! But that's what makes you who you are." Stephanie chuckled but then stopped when she saw a trance-like look on Alice's face.

"No, it's a pagoda I saw in the park. Unfortunately, I could never find it after that morning." Alice shook her head in amazement. Her whole being tingled with excitement.

"Please, Stephanie, will you set up a meeting with C.J. McGinnis as soon as possible? I wish I could explain this, but I can't. Not yet."

Alice gazed transfixed at remaining sketches spread before her—a pagoda, a fountain with three cherubs, an old-fashioned park bench, pigeons eating bread crumbs, the whimsical figure of a small boy with a frog's face, and a beautiful mystical unicorn with a gleaming golden horn and sparkling silver-blue hooves. The creature pranced in front of a cave's dark entrance.

40

THE MEETING

The tattered grey umbrella lay on the floor by the window. Alice had carefully placed it where the upturned canopy would catch the morning sunlight from a large glass-paned east window. It was the first time she'd opened the umbrella in several weeks. When it snapped open she noticed one slight tear along one of the ribs. The upturned umbrella cast a shadow on the floor and a tiny beam of hazy morning sunbeams shone through the small tear, lighting a gleaming spot on the wooden oak boards. The patch of sunlight was big enough for Sweetie Pie to lie on the floor and soak up the beams as he nestled close to the umbrella. Alice thought her dog acted like a cat in the way he slept in any small patch of sun he could find. Alice wrote in the mornings in the small room she called My Silent Place—silent except for the tapping of her fingers on the keyboard and an occasional soft doggy snore from the little black and white mutt.

Alice glanced at the brass retro style alarm clock on her desk. Her habit was to set the clock for one hour, take a ten minute break and then reset the clock for another hour. Today she completed two rounds of writing and didn't want to stop. The words flowed from her. Her train of thoughts sharply focused on the beginning of the new book. *Yes, the umbrella always worked. Why did I doubt?*

Alice had fifteen minutes to finish her work before the appointment with Stephanie and C. J. McGinnis. It wasn't her preference to have a meeting at her apartment, but this time she had insisted on her place. Even Saturday mornings the hectic atmosphere of the publishing company could be frantic if Stephanie's staff was on a deadline. Her anticipation at meeting the artist who'd sent the haunting sketches consumed her. She lost sleep thinking about them and memories of her days in the park. Early yesterday morning she'd finally admitted to herself that this meeting had been preordained by the one who had given her the lucky grey umbrella.

When Alice opened the door thirty minutes after the scheduled time, Stephanie threw up her arms and gestured behind her.

"Here we are!"

Alice knew that Stephanie never apologized for her tardiness. Behind her stood a slender young woman with dark kohl rimmed eyes. She was dressed in a sleeveless pale linen dress that accented her beautiful creamy brown skin.

"Alice, meet our mysterious artist! C. J. McGinnis." Stephanie stepped back and tried to usher the woman in the door. C. J. McGinnis stood and stared at Alice in an odd way and did not step forward.

"Alice Mason, known to her public as Marilee Mason, talented and rising star, why don't you ask us in?" Stephanie pushed her way through the doorway as Alice moved to the side.

Stephanie loved to speak in glowing terms when she introduced her authors. The practice had embarrassed Alice on more than one occasion.

"I'm so sorry. What am I thinking? Please, please do come in." Alice stammered.

Alice waved toward three chairs arranged around her writing table. She'd earlier cleared the desk's surface and arranged neat stacks of papers over the cramped floor space.

"Excuse the mess. I like to keep all my papers where I can see them. Great system, huh? I'm grateful you could come to my apartment. Hope it wasn't too much out of your way. Well, C. J., I'm very happy to meet you."

"Please, call me Carol. I'm only C. J. professionally." She sounded unsure of herself as if she needed to make a great effort to please Alice and Stephanie.

"Sure, sure. I understand that. Never thought I would be known as Marilee Mason, but my editor here thought that sounded like a great pen name." Alice paused before continuing what she hoped was a warm welcome for timid Carol.

"We're both impressed with your artwork."

"Alice, tell her what you told me! About how you recognized the settings and the people. You even believed one of the drawings was of you!" Stephanie could not contain herself and plunged into territory Alice had planned to explore after they had talked at more length.

"I can't wait to hear how all this came about. I'm sure it'll be great for sales of the new series! So how did you know to submit drawings of places and people Alice knew? It was a brilliant angle to play to get the interview, sweetheart." Stephanie thought everyone had an angle to play.

"I wasn't playing an angle." Carol's voice was soft but determined. "I just knew they were the right ones."

"What do you mean? What made you know they were the right ones?"

"Ms. Mason..." Carol started to speak but Alice interrupted with a smile.

"Don't call me Ms. Mason. I'm Alice."

"Someone told me several years ago that I would know the right time to show these drawings of the park and the people I saw there. I knew it was the right time. The person by the pagoda must have been you that day, that Saturday, remember?"

Alice was astounded. "Are you the girl I saw that morning when I last saw..." Alice's words trailed off. "Yes, you had a pad and were drawing the black woman with the ribbons in her hair."

"Yes, that's Bea. Bea Strickland. Do you want me to tell you about her?" Carol brightened up with a great smile.

Stephanie's cell phone began ringing, playing a loud rap song.

"Oh damn, you girls continue. I really have to take this. Very important! When I get done you've got to fill me in on all these coincidences of your past lives. Ha! Sounds like a novel to me!" Stephanie rushed out into the hallway to take her important call.

A long silence filled the room until Alice spoke. "Yes, Angel told me she talked to Bea and Carol, the others I saw that day. You are that Carol!"

"Who?" Carol seemed baffled by the name Angel, but Alice was putting it all together.

"Will you tell me how you know the woman Bea?"

"I know Bea really well. She's not in good health. Her daughter Florence came from California to take care of her. I go to visit as often as I can. I feel like she's an older aunt I always wished I'd had. She loves it when I call her Aunt Bea. You know, I should take you to meet her. We'd compare our experiences in the park! We could even tell each other the stories we heard and what we learned. You did learn some lessons, too, right? I learned to be brave and accept a new situation when I had to move and start in a new school."

"Yes, Carol. I learned some lessons. I even put many into practice. I acted to change my life. I left grad school and took writing courses. Something I'd always wanted to do."

"Bea always told me I would figure it all out one

day. Seems like we were destined to meet this way, huh? Bea told me she learned to be happy, to reach out to others. I've learned that I can face challenges, like trying to have a career in art. I guess I'll see how that works out."

"I know it will work out for you. Your sketches are fabulous and just what I need for my new series. We'll be working together." Alice felt as if her whole body was filled with air and that she might float away and change into large bubble of sheer happiness. "Tell me more about how you met Bea."

"After that one week in the park, I went to the Girls Club after school. My mom and I moved to a smaller apartment away from the park. One day Bea showed up for the art class. She had volunteered to help girls in the program. She even brought her friend, a neighbor lady, Miss Mamie, who taught arts and crafts for poor kids in the projects a long time ago. Miss Mamie had very bad eyesight; but between the two of them, we had great classes. After several months I showed Bea the set of drawings I made in the park. She couldn't believe her eyes and said she has seen the pagoda, the bench and the fountain. She told me one day I would show them to the right person at the right time. Later we talked about the storyteller we had met in the park. It was really all very weird because she'd met Bounty, a kind Hispanic lady, and I'd listened to Charity, a very cool teenager I really admired. When we discovered that we'd heard similar stories, we couldn't figure it out. We agreed that something so amazing and mysterious would probably never happen again in our lifetimes. So what do you say to that?"

Carol was breathless after telling her story nonstop. It was suddenly very quiet in the apartment and they could hear Stephanie's loud phone voice out in the hallway even though the door was shut.

Alice didn't know how to respond. She stared out the window and tried to compose her thoughts. Then she looked over at the familiar grey object under the window, Angel's umbrella. Carol followed her gaze.

Stephanie burst into the room in her usual frantic way but stopped speechless when she saw Alice and Carol sitting so quietly, not speaking. They looked like a painting of two friends deep in thought and comfortable with the companionship they had found.

"Where did you get that old grey umbrella?" Carol spoke in a barely audible whisper.

Alice and Carol looked at each other in silence for several minutes, neither of them wanting to be the first to speak of what they both knew had brought them together.

41

THE TIME TO REMEMBER

Three days after the meeting with Stephanie, Alice and Carol got out of a Yellow Cab in front of Bea's apartment building. Both were giddy with anticipation. Carol grabbed Alice's hand and pulled her toward the front door so quickly that Alice dropped the notebook she carried. As she bent to retrieve it she asked, "Do you think Bea will mind if I write down a few things about our meetings in the park with the storyteller?"

"Of course not, she'll be thrilled. She was so very happy when I called and explained as best I could about our interview. I rambled on and on until she told me to save the rest until we all were together. I also talked to her daughter Florence to be sure that this was a good time for her to have visitors."

"We have so much to tell to each other. Let's talk about the storyteller first, OK? I'll explain to both of you what my storyteller Angel told me. It is truly amazing what happened to all of us. How long should we stay?"

Carol dashed up the front steps ahead of Alice and held open the heavy door.

"Let's see how it goes this first time, but I know Aunt Bea will want us to stay even if she gets tired out."

"Should I call her Aunt Bea like you do?"

"That's up to you. It's been what I've called her since our time at Girl's Club. Of course, that was when I was still in middle school and desperately needed her in my life. Now I feel like she's always been my friend. Lucky me that I met her then and now I know you!" Carol's face glowed as she rang the buzzer. "I don't ever remember being so excited since the day I graduated art school."

At the first buzzer sound, a beautiful woman with green eyes and midnight black curls flung the door open. She wore round red glasses that matched the gauzy flowered blouse she wore. She was over 6 feet tall and very fit.

"Welcome. I'm Florence. So glad you're here.

Mama has been beside herself that you'd be late or cancel. You are Alice, the author Carol told me about?"

"Yes, very happy to meet you. We both wouldn't miss this time with your mother for anything."

As the three women walked through the front room, Alice couldn't help but notice the large collection of antique salt and peppers shakers in a glass display case and the lovely art that hung on the walls. She immediately recognized one beautiful charcoal sketch of an old iron park bench that was obviously Carol's work. Her heart swelled with joy. On a window ledge sat a beautifully framed slightly out-of-focus photo of a little dog sitting on a red and blue plaid doggie bed. She took a second glance as the odd thought crossed her mind that the dog in the photo looked like the same type black and white spotted mutt as her own Sweetie Pie.

"Mama, they're here," Florence spoke cheerfully to her mother who sat in the large armchair by the window. Although she was thinner and had aged considerably, Alice recognized at once the pink and red beribboned braids around the smiling face of the person she'd seen with Angel on a November Saturday ten years ago.

"All together now, aren't we? I'm so happy you're

here, Alice. I had almost given up hope that Carol and I would ever find the other person from that day. I didn't know anyone else was there until I saw Carol's sketch of a jogger by the pagoda. Please sit with me and we can start with our stories. Tell me about the person who told you the stories." Bea nodded toward the two wooden dining room chairs placed as closely as possible to the window where she sat.

After an hour and a half of conversation interspersed with laughter, Alice, Carol, and Bea finally stopped talking. Each had described in detail the different storytellers they had met. Florence interrupted once when she brought a tray of herb flavored tea and blueberry scones. All three sat in quiet contentment for several moments as Carol finished the last bites of her scone. Alice and Bea gazed out the window watching three pigeons, two large iridescent greys with darker wings and one smaller pure white one perched stoically in the sycamore tree next to the building. Large green leaves fluttered and the branches slightly swayed, yet the pigeons sat perfectly still, unfazed by the light breeze that blew through the tree.

"Now that Alice told us about why we all saw a different storyteller, I think I finally understand how much we were all helped by our experiences in the park," said Carol. "At that age, I probably wouldn't have stayed around to listen to anyone but a hip teen. It made me feel comfortable since she was mixed race like me. I was very sensitive and awkward about that as a kid. Aunt Bea, aren't you glad you found a friend to talk to? It all makes sense that we saw who we needed at the time."

Bea cleared her throat and intently looked at both Alice and Carol.

"One thing I haven't shared is a very strange experience I had on the fourth day. I got lost in the park and stumbled on an old fountain with three faceless baby angels. The sight of those ruined faces made me very unhappy. But I was always unhappy back then and couldn't see anything good about my life. It's different now for me. Anyway, I passed out or something. I woke up at the bench with my friend Bounty, I mean The Storyteller."

"You got lost before you saw the fountain? The same thing happened to me. I think it was on Thursday, the fourth day, now that you mention it." Alice swallowed hard after she spoke. "The fountain I saw had two angels with faces and one with a missing face. I fainted or something and woke up by the bench. Angel told me that she found me taking a nap on the grass. I thought about it later and decided that one with no face meant my future was not clear at that time. It was a bad time for me. I was about to get kicked out of grad school! But I never discussed that with The Storyteller. When Carol submitted the sketch of the fountain with three cherubs to Stephanie, I was speechless and puzzled. Carol, what happened with you?"

Carol looked with astonishment at both Alice and Bea. She tried not to laugh and shook her head. "Can you believe it? Guess we all should believe by now. I got lost on my way to the bench one day, too, and was really scared until I saw the fountain with the little angels and sat down to draw it. Then I felt dizzy. I always close my eyes and try to breathe when I get dizzy or afraid. When I opened my eyes, Charity was there. We were at the bench. I showed her the drawing, too. She said I'd had an inspiration. The cute statues I saw all had faces. A smiling face, a surprised face, and a praying face. Do you suppose that meant I was just a kid and had all my hopes intact for the future? I'd not thought about it like that until just now."

Alice, Bea, and Carol held each other's hands as the grandfather clock in the corner ticked several minutes away. Each one had a wistful smile on her face and tears in their eyes.

Florence entered the room quietly and spoke, "Mama, you really need to rest now while I fix your lunch. Do you all want to join us for a little sandwich?"

Alice and Carol looked at each other knowing that Florence was being polite with her invitation.

"No, no. We must go for today. Thanks for letting us come. We overstayed our time. We'll come every day next week starting on Monday like we promised." Turning toward Bea with a fond look, Alice said, "We'll retell every story we heard. Thanks again. So nice to meet you, Florence. Have a good weekend, Bea."

42

THE TIME FOR STORYTELLING

The apartment door opened before Alice could ring.

"I saw you all get out of the cab. I've been watching at the window." The tall woman who stood in the doorway had stress lines on her brow and puffy eyes like she hadn't slept all night.

"Florence, you look terrible. Has something happened to Bea?"

Alice and Carol had arrived earlier than their usual time because of a noon meeting to complete the marketing timeline plan for the new books. Stephanie insisted on Friday meetings, and always at the lunch hour. Alice carried a bulging briefcase filled with a ream of typed manuscript. Carol's faded red backpack brimmed with pencils and sketch pads.

They were ready for another session with Bea to recall their experiences in the park; all week they'd retold the stories to each other while Alice recorded and took notes. Carol did quick sketches of different scenes as they retold the versions they'd each heard. After their time together, Alice often worked late into the night to craft the compelling stories.

"She took a turn for the worse after you left yesterday afternoon. I didn't call because I thought she needed more rest, but she didn't rest at all. She kept me up almost all night talking about day five and a circus. For a while she sounded rational but later what she said made less and less sense. I put a call into the doctor, but I know what he'll say."

Carol gasped, but Alice pursed her lips and asked, "Do you think it's another mini-stoke?"

"Whatever it is, she wants to stay home. She's told me over and over not to take her back to the hospital. Please, come on back to her room. She's better now and has been asking when you'd be here. Does this talk about a numbered day and a circus make any sense to you?"

"Yes, it makes sense. It's the last day of the stories we all heard. Day five was Friday." Carol's eyes were misting over. She touched Alice's hand as they entered the bedroom.

Bea was propped up in the four poster bed. The pink and red ribbons on her small braids gave her a halo of bright color. A big smile came to her face when she saw them.

"What took you both so long to get here this afternoon?" Bea sounded weak. "Oh my goodness, it is only morning, isn't it? I get confused. But you're here now. We can start on day five." The hint of impatience in Bea's voice made Carol smile.

"Now Aunt Bea, don't you go getting grumpy on us."

"Not me. I'm over being grumpy. I gave that up years ago."

Usually Florence left the room when the two friends came to visit her mother; but this time, Alice motioned for her to stay and sit with them. Three chairs were pulled up beside the large bed, and Alice turned on the lamp so Carol would have enough light for her sketches. Florence had been told about Alice's manuscript and that Carol was illustrating the planned series of books.

"Let's begin, girls. The circus story was my favorite. Why don't you start this time, Carol. You shouldn't go last again just because you always went to the park later in the day than Alice and me," said Bea with an air of authority.

As Carol began retelling the story about *The Show of One Hundred Tricks,* Bea's palpable contentment filled the room. Bea chuckled out loud when Carol told about Chun Tao's cakes landing on the stage around Wen, the Chinese storyteller.

Moments later Florence looked worriedly at Alice and Carol when she saw her mother's head slowly drop and her eyes close.

"Mama, wake up and listen to the story. Maybe I should get you some tea. Would you like that? You all keep going. I'll be back with in a minute." Florence rose abruptly and walked into the kitchen. The sounds of water running and the teapot being placed on the stove echoed down the short hallway

"Bea, Bea. We're here. Carol finished her story. Will you tell us Bounty's story, the one about the circus. Can you do that?" Alice gently took Bea's hand as Carol pulled her chair closer to the bed, sketch pad on her lap and charcoal pencil in her hand. Bea's eyes opened but her gaze was unfocused and looked beyond the two women toward the window light.

"Yes, Bounty's story. The circus. My favorite." Bea tried to push herself up higher on the pillows. "Blanca joined the circus after she met Jose. He was a storyteller just like Bounty. Nice turn to the story.

Bounty's mamá made people laugh. Yes, that's how it went."

Alice looked at Carol with alarm as Bea laid her head back on white pillows and closed her eyes again.

"Rest, Bea. You don't have to talk right now. Florence is bringing tea. We'll finish the story later." Alice's hand trembled as she grabbed Carol's arm and they both leaned closer to Bea.

Sounds came from the kitchen of a teacup's rattle on a metal tray. A tree branch rustled as it brushed against the wall outside the open window. A siren wailed from a distant street. The fluttering sound of a white pigeon's wings caught Alice and Carol's attention as the bird landed on the outside window ledge and pecked on the wood three times. They both looked back at Bea when she coughed softly, opened her eyes, and strained to speak.

"My friends. Thanks for coming. Good stories. We learned the lessons. I'm joining the circus."

The white pigeon on the ledge bobbed her head and flew away.

THE END OF THE BEGINNING ONCE AGAIN

What we call the beginning is often the end. And to make an end is to make a beginning. The end is where we start from.

-T.S. Eliot

ABOUT THE AUTHOR

Jessica Lyn Elkins grew up in a small town in the Texas Panhandle. She moved to New Mexico in 1968 with her husband and two young children. She earned a BA in Geography and Biology from the University of New Mexico and graduated from St. John's College in Santa Fe, New Mexico with a Master of Arts in Liberal Education. A varied career path included stints as a general contractor, ice cream shop owner and human resources manager for multi-line automobile dealerships. Jessica Lyn and her husband Richard relocated to Gainesville, Florida in 2010. Her first novel The Friend in Question, a story of friendship and fateful coincidences, was published in 2015. A Coyote Taught Me Poetry, a collection of poetry and short prose, was completed in 2016. She finds inspiration for her writing in the diversity of the natural world and the complexity of human relationships.

ACKNOWLEDGEMENTS

My husband Dick convinced me I could be a storyteller. Without his love and infinite patience, the story would never have been told.

Peas in a Pod Fiction Critique Group members: Jane Camerlengo, Pat Caren, Richard Gartee, Skipper Hammond, Kimberly Mullins, and Joyce Southwell. These wonderful and wise friends are accomplished writers who advised, edited, laughed, and labored with me to complete The Storyteller's tales.

Good friends Diane Cordes, Becky DeMarie, Gwen McKinney, Phoebe Papádi, and my beloved niece Deidre Podlesnik were enlisted as first draft readers. They helped me to improve the story with their thoughtful suggestions. Fellow Scrabble players Diane Gillespie and Barb Frentzen reviewed later drafts and encouraged me in the last tedious days of revisions.

My publisher Karen Porter of Everfield Press gave me confidence and support. She believed in my story. We became friends in the process.

THE STORYTELLER IN THE PARK